THE CASE OF THE MONJA BLANCA

Volume 2: Zen and the Art of Investigation

ANTHONY WOLFF

authorHOUSE®

AuthorHouse™ LLC
1663 Liberty Drive
Bloomington, IN 47403
www.authorhouse.com
Phone: 1-800-839-8640

This is a work of fiction. All of the characters, names, incidents, organizations, and dialogue
in this novel are either the products of the author's imagination or are used fictitiously.

Published by AuthorHouse 02/21/2014

ISBN: 978-1-4918-5522-5 (sc)
ISBN: 978-1-4918-5533-1 (e)

Dedicated to Jessica L. F.

PREFACE

WHO ARE THESE DETECTIVES ANYWAY?

"The eye cannot see itself" an old Zen adage informs us. The Private I's in these case files count on the truth of that statement. People may be self-concerned, but they are rarely self-aware.

In courts of law, guilt or innocence often depends upon its presentation. Juries do not - indeed, they may not - investigate any evidence in order to test its veracity. No, they are obliged to evaluate only what they are shown. Private Investigators, on the other hand, are obliged to look beneath surfaces and to prove to their satisfaction - not the court's - whether or not what appears to be true is actually true. The Private I must have a penetrating eye.

Intuition is a spiritual gift and this, no doubt, is why *Wagner & Tilson, Private Investigators* does its work so well.

At first glance the little group of P.I.s who solve these often baffling cases seem different from what we (having become familiar with video Dicks) consider "sleuths." They have no oddball sidekicks. They are not alcoholics. They get along well with cops.

George Wagner is the only one who was trained for the job. He obtained a degree in criminology from Temple University in Philadelphia and did exemplary work as a investigator with the Philadelphia Police. These were his golden years. He skied; he danced; he played tennis; he had a Porsche, a Labrador retriever, and a small sailboat. He got married and had a wife, two toddlers, and a house. He was handsome and well built, and he had great hair.

And then one night, in 1999, he and his partner walked into an ambush. His partner was killed and George was shot in the left knee and in his right shoulder's brachial plexus. The pain resulting from his injuries and the twenty-two surgeries he endured throughout the year that followed, left him addicted to a nearly constant morphine drip. By the time he was admitted to a rehab center in Southern California for treatment of his morphine addiction and for physical therapy, he had lost everything previously mentioned except his house, his handsome face, and his great hair.

His wife, tired of visiting a semi-conscious man, divorced him and married a man who had more than enough money to make child support payments unnecessary and, since he was the jealous type, undesirable. They moved far away, and despite the calls George placed and the money and gifts he sent, they soon tended to regard him as non-existent. His wife did have an orchid collection which she boarded with a plant nursery, paying for the plants' care until he was able to accept them. He gave his brother his car, his tennis racquets, his skis, and his sailboat.

At the age of thirty-four he was officially disabled, his right arm and hand had begun to wither slightly from limited use, a frequent result of a severe injury to that nerve center. His knee, too, was troublesome. He could not hold it in a bent position for an extended period of time; and when the weather was bad or he had been standing for too long, he limped a little.

George gave considerable thought to the "disease" of romantic love and decided that he had acquired an immunity to it. He would never again be vulnerable to its delirium. He did not realize that the gods of love regard such pronouncements as hubris of the worst kind and, as such, never allow it to go unpunished. George learned this lesson while working on the case, *The Monja Blanca*. A sweet girl, half his age and nearly half his weight, would fell him, as he put it, "as young David slew the big dumb Goliath." He understood that while he had no future with her, his future would be filled with her for as long as he had a mind that could think. She had been the victim of the most vicious swindlers he had ever encountered. They had successfully fled the country, but not the range of George's determination to apprehend them. These were master criminals, four of them, and he secretly vowed that he would make them fall, one by one. This was a serious quest. There was nothing quixotic about George Roberts Wagner.

While he was in the hospital receiving treatment for those fateful gunshot wounds, he met Beryl Tilson.

Beryl, a widow whose son Jack was then eleven years old, was working her way through college as a nurse's aid when she tended George. She had met him previously when he delivered a lecture on the curious differences between aggravated assault and attempted murder, a not uninteresting topic. During the year she tended him, they became friendly enough for him to communicate with her during the year he was in rehab. When he returned to Philadelphia, she picked him up at the airport, drove him home - to a house he had not been inside for two years - and helped him to get settled into a routine with the house and the botanical spoils of his divorce.

After receiving her degree in the Liberal Arts, Beryl tried to find a job with hours that would permit her to be home when her son came home from school each day. Her quest was daunting. Not only was a degree in Liberal Arts regarded as a 'negative' when considering an applicant's qualifications, (the choice of study having demonstrated a lack of foresight for eventual entry into the commercial job market) but by stipulating that she needed to be home no later than 3:30 p.m. each day, she further discouraged personnel managers from putting out their company's welcome mat. The supply of available jobs was somewhat limited.

Beryl, a Zen Buddhist and karate practitioner, was still doing part-time work when George proposed that they open a private investigation agency. Originally he had thought she would function as a "girl friday" office manager; but when he witnessed her abilities in the martial arts, which, at that time, far exceeded his, he agreed that she should function as a 50-50 partner in the agency, and he helped her through the licensing procedure. She quickly became an excellent marksman on the gun range. As a Christmas gift he gave her a Beretta to use alternately with her Colt semi-automatic.

The Zen temple she attended was located on Germantown Avenue in a two storey, store-front row of small businesses. Wagner & Tilson, Private Investigators needed a home. Beryl noticed that a building in the same row was advertised for sale. She told George who liked it, bought it, and let Beryl and her son move into the second floor as their residence. Problem solved.

While George considered himself a man's man, Beryl did not see herself as a woman's woman. She had no female friends her own age. None. Acquaintances, yes. She enjoyed warm relationships with a few older women. But Beryl, it surprised her to realize, was a man's woman. She liked men, their freedom to move, to create, to discover, and that inexplicable wildness that came with their physical presence and strength. All of her senses found them agreeable; but she had no desire to domesticate one. Going to sleep with one was nice. But waking up with one of them in her bed? No. No. No. Dawn had an alchemical effect on her sensibilities. "Colors seen by candlelight do not look the same by day," said Elizabeth Barrett Browning, to which Beryl replied, "Amen."

She would find no occasion to alter her orisons until, in the course of solving a missing person's case that involved sexual slavery in a South American rainforest, a case called *Skyspirit*, she met the Surinamese Southern District's chief criminal investigator. Dawn became conducive to romance. But, as we all know, the odds are always against the success of long distance love affairs. To be stuck in one continent and love a man who is stuck in another holds as much promise for high romance as falling in love with Dorian Gray. In her professional life, she was tough but fair. In matters of lethality, she preferred *dim mak* points to bullets, the latter being awfully messy.

Perhaps the most unusual of the three detectives is Sensei Percy Wong. The reader may find it useful to know a bit more about his background.

Sensei, Beryl's karate master, left his dojo to go to Taiwan to become a fully ordained Zen Buddhist priest in the Ummon or Yun Men lineage in which he was given the Dharma name Shi Yao Feng. After studying advanced martial arts in both Taiwan and China, he returned to the U.S.

to teach karate again and to open a small Zen Buddhist temple - the temple that was down the street from the office *Wagner & Tilson* would eventually open.

Sensei was quickly considered a great martial arts' master not because, as he explains, "I am good at karate, but because I am better at advertising it." He was of Chinese descent and had been ordained in China, and since China's Chan Buddhism and Gung Fu stand in polite rivalry to Japan's Zen Buddhism and Karate, it was most peculiar to find a priest in China's Yun Men lineage who followed the Japanese Zen liturgy and the martial arts discipline of Karate.

It was only natural that Sensei Percy Wong's Japanese associates proclaimed that his preferences were based on merit, and in fairness to them, he did not care to disabuse them of this notion. In truth, it was Sensei's childhood rebellion against his tyrannical faux-Confucian father that caused him to gravitate to the Japanese forms. Though both of his parents had emigrated from China, his father decried western civilization even as he grew rich exploiting its freedoms and commercial opportunities. With draconian finesse he imposed upon his family the cultural values of the country from which he had fled for his life. He seriously believed that while the rest of the world's population might have come out of Africa, Chinese men came out of heaven. He did not know or care where Chinese women originated so long as they kept their proper place as slaves.

His mother, however, marveled at American diversity and refused to speak Chinese to her children, believing, as she did, in the old fashioned idea that it is wise to speak the language of the country in which one claims citizenship.

At every turn the dear lady outsmarted her obsessively sinophilic husband. Forced to serve rice at every meal along with other mysterious creatures obtained in Cantonese Chinatown, she purchased two Shar Peis that, being from Macau, were given free rein of the dining room. These dogs, despite their pre-Qin dynasty lineage, lacked a discerning palate and proved to be gluttons for bowls of fluffy white stuff. When her husband retreated to his rooms, she served omelettes and Cheerios, milk instead of tea, and at dinner, when he was not there at all, spaghetti instead of chow mein. The family home was crammed with gaudy enameled furniture and torturously carved teak; but on top of the lion-head-ball-claw-legged coffee table, she always placed a book which illustrated the elegant simplicity of such furniture designers as Marcel Breuer; Eileen Gray; Charles Eames; and American Shakers. Sensei adored her; and loved to hear her relate how, when his father ordered her to give their firstborn son a Chinese name; she secretly asked the clerk to record indelibly the name "Percy" which she mistakenly thought was a very American name. To Sensei, if she had named him Abraham Lincoln Wong, she could not have given him a more Yankee handle.

Preferring the cuisines of Italy and Mexico, Sensei avoided Chinese food and prided himself on not knowing a word of Chinese. He balanced this ignorance by an inability to understand Japanese and, because of its inaccessibility, he did not eat Japanese food.

The Man of Zen who practices Karate obviously is the adventurous type; and Sensei, staying true to type, enjoyed participating in Beryl's and George's investigations. It required little time for him to become a one-third partner of the team. He called himself, "the ampersand in *Wagner & Tilson*."

Sensei Wong may have been better at advertising karate than at performing it, but this merely says that he was a superb huckster for the discipline. In college he had studied civil engineering; but he also was on the fencing team and he regularly practiced gymnastics. He had learned yoga and ancient forms of meditation from his mother. He attained Zen's vaunted transcendental states which he could access 'on the mat.' It was not surprising that when he began to learn karate he was already half-accomplished. After he won a few minor championships he attracted the attention of several martial arts publications that found his "unprecedented" switchings newsworthy. They imparted to him a "great master" cachet, and perpetuated it to the delight of dojo owners and martial arts shopkeepers. He did win many championships and, through unpaid endorsements and political propaganda, inspired the sale of Japanese weapons, including nunchaku and shuriken which he did not actually use.

Although his Order was strongly given to celibacy, enough wiggle room remained for the priest who found it expedient to marry or dally. Yet, having reached his mid-forties unattached, he regarded it as 'unlikely' that he would ever be romantically welded to a female, and as 'impossible' that he would be bonded to a citizen and custom's agent of the People's Republic of China - whose Gung Fu abilities challenged him and who would strike terror in his heart especially when she wore Manolo Blahnik red spike heels. Such combat, he insisted, was patently unfair, but he prayed that Providence would not level the playing field. He met his femme fatale while working on A Case of Virga.

Later in their association Sensei would take under his spiritual wing a young Thai monk who had a degree in computer science and a flair for acting. Akara Chatree, to whom Sensei's master in Taiwan would give the name Shi Yao Xin, loved Shakespeare; but his father - who came from one of Thailand's many noble families - regarded his son's desire to become an actor as we would regard our son's desire to become a hit man. Akara's brothers were all businessmen and professionals; and as the old patriarch lay dying, he exacted a promise from his tall 'matinee-idol' son that he would never tread upon the flooring of a stage. The old man had asked for nothing else, and since he bequeathed a rather large sum of money to his young son, Akara had to content himself with critiquing the performances of actors who were less filially constrained than he. As far as romance is concerned, he had not thought too much about it until he worked on A Case of Industrial Espionage. That case took him to Bermuda, and what can a young hero do when he is captivated by a pretty girl who can recite Portia's lines with crystalline insight while lying beside him on a white beach near a blue ocean?

But his story will keep...

WEDNESDAY, JANUARY 13, 2010

In January the sun had begun in earnest its slow shift to the north, affecting the angle at which light struck George's "hospitalized" plants in the storefront window. It was time to rearrange them, to wash the window, inside and out, and to put new yellow plastic sheeting against the glass. George was therefore in the perfect position, as well as the somewhat awkward one, to see the cream colored limousine pull up to the curb.

He stood on the raised display platform, Windex bottle in hand, and whispered, "Uh, oh." Beryl looked up from her desk. Through the office door's long glass pane she could see the liveried chauffeur get out of the driver's seat and walk to the sidewalk to open the car's rear door and assist an elegantly dressed woman of about fifty to step out. She wore a black wide brimmed hat and black wool suit, both trimmed with black satin, and she carried a long gold-handled walking stick as she crossed the pavement and approached the office. The chauffeur closed the car door, and as she tapped the office door with the metal tip of the stick, he quickly crossed to reach around her to open it.

As she entered, George stepped down awkwardly from the display window. An old gunshot wound to his knee prevented a more graceful descent.

Speaking in a slightly French accent, the lady directed her chauffeur, "Eric, if it's necessary to move the car, I'll telephone you when I'm ready to leave." He clicked his heels together and stepped forward to extend a calling card to Beryl who took it by its edges and stared at it as though it were a ransom note. It read, "Charlotte LaFontaine, Contesse deLisle" in gold engraved letters.

"Won't you sit down, Countess," Beryl said, unaccustomed to using such a title. She noticed a small red shield pinned to the countess's lapel. As the woman sat down Beryl was able to distinguish a Maltese cross in the center of the cloisonne pin.

The Countess peered up at George from beneath her hat brim. She asked, "And you are?"

"I'm half of Wagner and Tilson. The George Wagner half."

"Then you are the half I came to see," she said, unamused by his attempt at humor.

Beryl stood up and gave the card to George. "Use my desk. I have work to do in the back, anyway."

George studied the card as he sat down. "And what can I do for you, Madame?"

"I'll be brief. Alicia Eckersley recommended you for a very delicate task. Do you know Mrs. Eckersley?"

"Yes. I'm happy to hear that she spoke well of me."

"We recently met at a reception for the President of France... in Washington."

George nodded as though the remark were meaningful. "Ah, I see," he said.

"My son, Henri, has fallen in love with an American girl of the Smith family. Do you know them? They are... confectioners... candy makers."

"I'm not sure I know those specific Smiths. We have many Smiths."

"The father is Everett Post Smith. The mother is Cecelia Tarleton Smith."

"Ah," said George with relief. "I do know those Smiths. They raise orchids."

"Exactly. It was regarding orchids that Mrs. Eckersley recommended you."

"They have a famous collection at their estate in Bryn Mawr, out on the Main Line."

"I have seen this Main Line. Very pretty, in a bourgeois sort of way... the homes of merchants and professionals. Someone who has a hundred acres calls it an estate."

"Yes, a hundred acres qualifies as... well.. yes. What specifically did you have in mind?"

"My son will inherit several estates. Places of note in France, Austria, and Germany that one can point to on a map. Do you understand?"

"I think so."

"So, Mr. Wagner, who is this girl... this Lilyanne Smith who has captivated my son? Her name is the first word he speaks when he wakes at dawn. Her name is the last word he speaks when he retires at night. And he does not utter two consecutive sentences during the day without her name being mentioned in one of them."

George shrugged his shoulders. "Sounds like he's in love."

"Obsessed would be precise. Such love makes a man foolish, generous, weak. I know how passionate the men of my family can be... how reckless they can become when they are unrestrained. I need to know. Who is this Lilyanne Smith person? Who are these candy makers?"

"How did your son meet her?"

"She was introduced to him last October at the Matisse exhibit at the Philadelphia Art Museum. He was instantly enamored. He wants to marry her." Bewildered, the countess raised her manicured and ring-decorated fingers to her temples. George knew enough of diamonds to see that hers were large and genuine.

"How does she feel about him?"

The countess grew angry. "Of what significance is that? Who is she? He tells me that she's been in a convent, close to taking her final vows as a nun. I like that, of course. I insist that my son marry a virgin. We are a family of strict Roman Catholics. I want no sordid histories disrupting the integrity of our lineage."

Still wondering what any of this had to do with him, George allowed himself to be dragged through the conversation. "Why did she leave the convent?"

"We're told that she left at the insistence of her parents. It seems that her brother, the family's only other child, was killed in an automobile accident. Her parents wanted her to return to secular life. I suppose they want her to carry on the name of.... Smith."

"Well, this particular Smith family is supposed to be wealthy. Maybe they wanted grandchildren to leave their money to."

"This is my problem. Suppositions and worthless talk. What do we really have here? A *parvenu*? Is hers a family of opportunists? Do they truly have wealth? Are they established or merely *nouveau riche*? Is this girl an adventuress? How do we know where she's been for the last five years? She's twenty-three yet no one in society seems to know anything about her. A convent? Perhaps that is a pretty way of saying 'asylum' or worse. She limps. Yes, limps. And she has burn scars. Perhaps she was in an accident and cannot bear children. Perhaps the injury caused her to become addicted to narcotics. We have heard all kinds of gossip. We simply do not know."

"How," asked George, "does my familiarity with orchids help you with these questions? The financial investigation is a simple matter; but medical issues are subject to laws of privacy. We can't go to her physician and ask him about the status of her reproductive organs."

"No you can't. But what you can do is to keep your eyes and ears open, and to use your professional skills of observation and sly interrogation to learn what the true history is. Mrs. Smith happened to mention that the man in charge of her hothouse had unexpectedly retired. She asked Alicia Eckersley if she knew of an orchid expert - evidently their collection is extensive and valuable. Mrs. Eckersley mentioned your name but doubted that you would accept the position since orchids were merely your hobby, your profession being that of a private investigator. When I heard this my soul rejoiced. It was the perfect solution. I could barely contain my hopes. Now, if you would accept the position…"

Finally, he understood the nature of the case. "I can apply for it," he said.

"I have asked my son to be direct and to ask Miss Smith whether or not she can have children. But he refuses. He says that she is a virgin and it would not be proper to ask her or her parents such a question. In Europe, we would ask without reservation. So you see the need for subterfuge. I would like you to contact her as soon as possible and in the course of conversation you could casually mention that you'd like to devote more of your time to horticulture and make it your vocation rather than your avocation."

George tried to imagine himself casually making such a statement. The image struck him funny and he smiled. "An undercover orchidologist.

Frankly, I like it. Let's see whether the position is available." He went into his office and returned with a copy of *The Orchid Digest*. "I'll make a few brief calls and get right back to you. Perhaps you'd enjoy looking through this while I attend to the calls."

He signaled Beryl that they should go upstairs to her apartment. He wanted the calls to be made in private.

Inside her apartment, he said, "I don't know if Alicia Eckersley will go along with this, but call her and ask if she'll call Cecelia Smith and find out if I can apply for the greenhouse job. If I can, set up a job interview and call me at your desk. If she doesn't want to call Cecelia, call and tell me that you couldn't reach her." George waited until Beryl got Alicia on the line. He returned to the Countess.

Alicia remembered the conversation in Washington. "That woman," she said emphatically, "is insufferable." She could readily understand what "the mission" was. "She wants George to spy on the Smiths while he's working in the hothouse. She wants me to help him get the job by putting in a good word for him with Cecelia. And I imagine that woman is sitting in your office now. I'll call Cecelia right away and call you back, and then later, when she's not there, I'll tell you about poor Lilyanne who's going to be stuck with her for a mother-in-law. You be sure to call me back when Her Highness leaves."

Beryl put a load of laundry in the washer while she waited for Alicia Eckersley to complete "the mission."

In ten minutes, Alicia called. "Cecelia Smith is what Lionel calls 'a buck passer.' She says that since I am recommending George as an orchid expert, he can have the job subject to her approval at an interview tomorrow morning at eleven o'clock at Tarleton House. She'll be waiting for him in the greenhouse. I'm certain that she'll give him the job. It is what Lionel calls a 'win-win' proposition for her. If he works out, she will be silently happy. And if he doesn't work out, she will be vocally happy, telling everyone how she should never have listened to me. Her happiness is assured in any event. She is a vile gossip. She really is. Now, be sure to call me back after that insufferable countess leaves and I'll tell you all about Lilyanne."

Beryl called the office phone which rang on her desk. When George answered she said, "You have an eleven o'clock interview tomorrow at Tarleton House. Alicia says you're a shoo-in."

George opened a desk drawer. "Apparently," he said to his new client, "I've got the position if I want it." He removed two contract forms and presented them to her. "We'll require a substantial retainer."

The contesse glanced at the agreement and began to fill in the black spaces. "Would twenty thousand dollars be sufficient?"

"Yes, it would,"George said.

She signed the contract and withdrew a checkbook from her handbag. "Your card, please."

The name *Wagner and Tilson, Private Investigators* was already printed on the contract, nevertheless George went back into his office and got his own card which she referred to as she wrote the check. "Now, from what I understand, the girl Lilyanne likes orchids. Get to know her. See if she's mentally sound. Mental illness can so easily be masked by pharmaceuticals. Gauge her character. Does she tend to exaggerate? Is she vain? Frivolous? Intelligent? In subtle ways, test her knowledge of Catholicism. Befriend her servants. Her maid will know if she menstruates regularly. Be alert! There are always clues, however slight, that indicate whether wealth is so much ink on paper or whether it is, in fact, substantial. Check newspaper files to see if there are criminals in the family. Visit pubs in the area and gossip a bit. I think I need not burden you with more suggestions."

George signed both copies of the contract and gave one to her. She placed the contract, her check book and George's card into her purse and stood up.

George asked, "Where can I reach you?"

"We are staying at The Declan."

George walked ahead to open the door for her.

Beryl returned to her desk. "I caught that *Order of Malta* pin on her lapel. She really pushes that Catholicism connection," Beryl laughed. "Are you up on your Catechism?"

"She didn't sound like a particularly spiritual woman to me," George said. "I just hope her check is as genuine as the diamonds she was wearing."

"Alicia is gonna give me the scoop on the girl. I can put her on speaker if you want to listen."

"Let me get a couple of iced teas from the back. This may take awhile."

Alicia Eckersley believed in prefaces. "No doubt when I met that countess-person," she began, "I was in a bad mood. Our flight had been delayed. We were going to Washington to attend the wedding of a girl I went to school with. After the reception we had to show up at some cocktail party given for one of those French diplomats. Even in the best of times... or maybe in the worst of times..."

George and Beryl looked at each other. George groaned and Beryl struggled to suppress a laugh.

Alicia continued. "All of the fun has gone out of flying," she whined. "It's like going to an abattoir. Lionel and I were poked, prodded, x-rayed, and rubbed with wands that meow like cats. I was carrying a wedding present - a *Waterford* vase. And wouldn't you know that lead crystal glows green like some explosive in their scanning machines, and we had airport security surround us like a SWAT team while I unpacked my bag and unwrapped the vase. Everyone backed away from us. I felt like a terrorist leper. All this for a girl I went to school with who is seventy-five years old and still insists on getting married in a long white gown. I thank God it wasn't strapless. A train. Beryl, she had a train. It must have been six feet long. I could understand the veil and the bouquet of calla lilies. I think she was rehearsing."

Beryl giggled. "For her wake?"

Alicia paused to think a moment. "I got the distinct impression that two of the groomsmen were paramedics. Maybe the bridesmaids were registered nurses. They could have had oxygen bottles under their bouquets.

"Lionel and I made an appearance at the reception and then we rushed on to the embassy party. That's why I probably wasn't in the best of moods.

"You know the kind of people you're dealing with when they speak a foreign language to you…. one that you studied a thousand years ago in school… and they speak it as fast as they possibly can. That is a clue to their personalities. Remember that, Beryl. It reveals character. So, there I was between the two of them… one trying to speak French faster than the other, with all those guttural and nasal sounds flying around. The countess played her Parisian accent ace. She looked straight down her nose at Cecelia. She didn't know that Cecelia Tarleton Smith had French nannies and went to French private schools and even attended the Sorbonne." Alicia paused. "I wonder… why didn't she know that? Anyway, that Sorbonne did the trick. Insisting that you've been privately tutored won't work next to that French school. The countess surrendered."

"How did she do that?" Beryl asked.

"She began to speak English! And the contest was over. She must be a fake. A true aristocrat wouldn't have talked too fast for me to understand. That was a clue. It wasn't that she was uneducated. I know lots of aristocrats who are barely literate. Cecelia's not a fake. She's nasty and doesn't pretend to be otherwise. Anyway, when they began to speak English, they condescended to include me. That's when the subject of orchids came up."

"What can you tell us about Lilyanne? George is particularly interested."

Alicia sighed. "It was horrible. It drove the girl right into a convent. And for all her mother cared, she would have stayed there till doomsday. But their only other child, Everett Junior, got himself killed driving drunk. They spoiled that boy rotten. I know people say we spoiled our boy; but we sent him to military school and then he had a career in the Army. Our Dalton was a lot of things, but he wasn't wild the way their son was. Not habitually, anyway.

"Anyway, it happened at a Fourth of July picnic. It was just before the century changed, so that would make it 1999. The Smiths had a big barbecue with at least a hundred guests. Everett Junior wanted to roast some jalapeno peppers which would have given off horrible fumes, so he was told to get an old three-legged barbecue stand from the basement to use off on the side someplace. Everett Junior didn't think the charcoal briquets were burning fast enough so he got a can of lighter fluid and started to squirt it into the burning coals. Lilyanne shouted, 'Don't do that!' He laughed, and she reached for the can to stop him, it exploded and she was burned all up and down her right side. But in the excitement people rushed to help and the barbecue stand got knocked over and Lilyanne got a load of burning briquets on her left foot. Even her hair was on fire. I tell you it was horrible.

"Someone had the presence of mind to turn on a nearby garden hose and squirt her. He kept the hose on her to cool down her body - which was the perfect thing to do the paramedics said. Nevertheless, she was in and out of the hospital getting skin grafts for nearly a year, I think it was."

George winced and grunted. In that same year George had walked into an ambush and was shot in his right shoulder and his left knee. He, too, spent a year in the hospital undergoing twenty-two surgeries. Permanently disabled, he retired as a police department investigator.

"Well," continued Alicia, "after the year in the hospital, she became a recluse at home for a few years; and then when she was eighteen she went into a convent. When Junior got killed last summer, they insisted that she come home. She was their genetic last resort, so to speak."

"Do you happen to know the name of the convent?" Beryl asked.

"Yes, I do. While I was waiting for you to call me back I asked my cook. It's the Sisters of Saint Catherine, Darminton, West Virginia. Servants gossip worse than we do. If you want true dirt, Beryl, talk to your cook."

Beryl laughed. "I'll remember that. Can you tell me anything more about them or their daughter?"

"No... except they're touchy people. No one could ever say a negative word about their son. Cecelia Smith even blamed Lilyanne for the accident. She told people, 'Everything was absolutely fine until she interfered.' A jackass knows you shouldn't squirt lighter fluid into flames. And Cecelia blames the sensible one who tried to prevent it. And their jackass son crashed his car into a maple tree. Thank God no one else was in the car and the maple will recover."

THURSDAY, JANUARY 14, 2010

Promptly at 10:45 a.m. George turned his pickup truck onto the Tarelton House private drive and was immediately stopped by a high gate and gatekeeper. He rolled down the window and called, "I'm George Wagner, here to interview for the hothouse job. Mrs. Smith is expecting me."

The gatekeeper, a thin old man who had to adjust his hearing aid to get the information, checked his log book and flipped the switch that electrically opened the gate.

George drove for a quarter mile before he turned off the road that led to the front of the mansion and followed the road that led back to the hothouse. He parked, and a servant of a rank George could not determine approached him.

"You are Wagner, I presume. I'm Sanford, the *major domo*. Mrs. Smith is waiting in the hothouse. Follow me."

Inside the glass structure grew orchids of varieties George had seen only in photographs. He made no effort to conceal his admiration.

Cecelia Tarleton Smith held herself as stiffly as an insulted monarch. It was a pose she always struck when interviewing someone for a job. In the event she decided not to hire George, it would make rejecting him much easier. She picked up a potted plant, looked at George and said, "*Trichopilia tortilis.* Beautiful, isn't it?"

George smiled slightly as if he were in on the joke. "It would be if it were, Madam; but I think it is *Trichopilia suavis*, a much more beautiful species, in my opinion."

"You're hired," she said simply. "A thousand a week to start?"

George nodded affirmatively.

Her tone of voice changed. She was suddenly snappish. "Your apartment is over the garage. The key should be on the table near the front door. The bed has a quality mattress. Sanford will order your rooms to be fitted with linens and towels. You can take your meals in the kitchen with the staff or, if you prefer, they can be delivered to your rooms or here in the hothouse. The housekeeper will see to the cleaning of your rooms and to your laundry. Your days off will be Monday and Tuesday." She turned to Sanford who was straightening papers on a desk in the hothouse vestibule. "Get his social security information for tax purposes. You know what we need." She returned to George. "When we entertain we require quality blooms that harmonize with the linen color. And we need our centerpieces to be esthetically pleasing and relevant to the occasion. Sanford will tell you what is required."

"Madame," George said politely, "I'd be pleased to make an arrangement now, subject to Sanford's guidance and approval, for your luncheon table, as a sample of my work."

Cecelia Tarleton Smith thought about it. "We're having trout for lunch. The table cloth will be yellow I believe. Good. I'm planning an extremely important dinner next week. Do your best."

As she walked out of the hothouse she glanced back at George. "Don't use anything rare. Use the phalaenopsis. We have plenty of them from before the time that hardware stores began to sell them."

Sanford rolled his eyes and followed her out.

George looked around to familiarize himself with the location of the thermostat, tools, plant supplies, and decorative pots and display items. As he looked out the window towards the house, he saw a girl coming towards the hothouse.

As he bent down to examine the contents of a cabinet, he caught the flash of movement at an outside corner of the hothouse. He waited a minute and then, for a reason he would never understand, called out, "Where is that darned cat!"

A pretty young girl peered at him from the corner. "Meow," she said, giggling.

George got down on his hands and knees and began to bark like a puppy. She stepped back and he crawled towards her, putting his head around the corner. "Yip, yip, yip, grrrrr." She squealed a playful laugh and began to run away, limping. He stood up and watched her. She had a mass of curly blonde hair, a few locks of which bounced over her ears, but he could still detect scars beneath the curls. She was wearing a sweater over her shoulders, and when she suddenly turned around to wave at him, the sweater fell back from her arm and he could see the scars there, too.

"So this is Lilyanne," George said aloud. In his eyes, she was adorable.

He walked back into the hothouse and began to look for a suitable bowl for the centerpiece. Without thinking about it, he decided to create a narrative arrangement. He selected yellow phalaenopsis orchids that were the exact color of her hair. He also found a white *Capanemia uliginosa* plant that was in a fairly shallow pot. The tall stalks of white flowers hung gracefully like a weeping willow tree. He found artificial rocks, peat moss, and from a box of decorative figurines, he picked two rabbits - one that was standing and looking down, and another that was sitting and looking up.

He placed the *Capanemia's* pot into the bowl, hiding it with peat moss and rocks. Then he created a landscape in which the grass was replaced with golden orchid blooms that he cut from the stems. One rabbit sat among the flowers and looked up at the other that was on a rocky ledge, looking down from between the draping orchid branches.

He typed on a card, "Grass that turned to beautiful golden orchids when it saw Lilyanne's hair and two bunnies that are in love."

Sanford read the card when he came to pick up the centerpiece. "It's quite nice," he said, "and so is the arrangement."

After introductions, George had lunch with the staff. He maintained a friendly attitude; and as he left he said goodbye to everyone individually, calling each by name which he had purposely memorized. He checked his two-room apartment over the garage, took the key from the table, locked the door and returned to the hothouse. Using the land line phone on his desk in the anteroom, he called Beryl. "I'm in," he said. "How will you get to the convent?"

"I'll drive. I'll call now and make an appointment. If the prioress agrees to see me tomorrow, I'll leave before dawn, see her and then check into a motel and drive home Saturday."

"Can you call Perce now and tell him I can't play shuffleboard tomorrow night. My days off are Mondays and Tuesdays. I officially start tomorrow."

"Did you see the girl?"

"Yes. She's adorable. What a kick in the ass to think of her being stuck between those two Battle-Axes."

Instead of going home, George decided to clean some of the greenhouse windows. As he stood outside wiping, he heard the uneven footsteps of his earlier visitor. He searched the glass to see if he could find her reflection. There was a large rhododendron bush some twenty feet away from the glass house. He heard a small voice coming from behind the bush. "Thank you for the centerpiece. I loved it. Everybody did." And again he heard the uneven footsteps, but now they faded away.

Late in the afternoon, he selected one of the two pubs that were in the vicinity. He ordered a sandwich and observed the clientele. They were business-like and as gossipers did not seem promising. He drove to the other pub and was surprised to see that there was a shuffleboard which was being played on by two teams. He stayed at the bar and within an hour, one team member left and his teammate asked if anyone wanted to play. George volunteered. For another hour he enjoyed himself while laying the groundwork for more serious conversation at a later time.

He left the bar at ten thirty and returned to his own house just north of Philadelphia. He ate some cheesecake, drank a glass of milk, took his evening sleep and arthritis medication, showered, brushed his teeth, and went to bed; but he could not sleep. At one o'clock he took a tranquilizer and finally fell asleep.

FRIDAY. JANUARY 15, 2010

The sky glowed a faint red in her rear view mirrors, but it was still dark when Beryl turned onto the Pennsylvania Turnpike and headed west. A thin fog limited the distance her headlights could illuminate, enclosing her in a colorless space. As the eastern sky grew lighter, the world on either side of the highway began to contain ghostly grey shapes. The dawn light grew into a bolder red, then brightened into orange and yellow until finally the sun broke the horizon to dazzle in her rear-view mirrors. In minutes, heat pulled the blanket of mist off the asphalt and the turnpike yawned and stretched out before her.

By seven o'clock, the morning was cold, clear, and sunny, and Beryl, cruising through Amish country, hummed and sang what lyrics she could remember from the musical, *Plain and Fancy*.

Eric, the chauffeur, sat up, scratched the stubble of his beard, and got out of Charlotte's bed. Naked, his body showed the perfect proportions that were obvious in his uniform and sleek knee-high boots. The toilet seat banged as he flipped it up, waking her. As he urinated he called out, "Order breakfast… and tell them to make sure the cantaloupe is ripe. Yesterday it was half green. And get me scrambled eggs. Their "over easy" eggs are more like hard boiled eggs out flat. And get more of those hash browns. They were good. And orange juice and a pot of tea. Darjeeling. Maybe a few croissants."

Charlotte La Fontaine, disheveled, reached for a cigarette and lighter on the bedside table. Her breasts sagged against the sheet as she supported herself on one elbow, took a deep drag on the cigarette, blew the smoke towards the ceiling and picked up a pen and hotel notepad. "Don't you want bacon?"

Eric shook off the last drops of urine. "No. I need to stay trim." He admired himself in the full length mirror on the bathroom door. "To hell with the bacon."

The Contesse finished writing his order. "And if the cantaloupe isn't ripe?" she called.

"Papaya or some other kind of ripe melon. Maybe a nice banana." He walked to the doorway of the other bedroom. "Henri! Martin! What do you want for breakfast?"

After a moment's mumbling, Henri called, "What you ordered is fine with us. But we'll have the bacon, too."

"All right, darling," Charlotte called. I'll get room service."

From the bedroom, Martin shouted, "And don't tie up the line picking and picking through their menu. I'm waiting on a call."

"All right. I'll just have what you ordered." She picked up the telephone and dialed room service.

"No!" Henri shouted. "Forget the bacon, Mammá. You've gained five pounds since D.C. You're starting to look like the Venus of Willendorf."

"You're a beast!" she had time to say before the Room Service clerk answered.

In the morning George packed a few changes of clothing, toiletries, and his prescription medicines in a sport bag and drove directly to Tarleton House. He unpacked in his little apartment over the garage and was ready to eat breakfast with the staff at 8 a.m.

The cook made an announcement. "I'm told that the wedding - if there is going to be a wedding - will be held in Saint Gregory's Cathedral."

"How far away is that?" George asked.

Sanford answered, "About twenty miles."

"Will we be supplying the flowers for the church?"

"No, but the reception will be held here. It won't be a big wedding. Miss Lilyanne has been away for a long time," said Sanford.

"The poor creature has no girlfriends... nobody, really," said the cook, "not even for a maid of honor."

George nodded. "So the wedding will mainly be for the parents."

Letty, the cook, was visibly upset. "I think Miss Lilyanne is so shy that she would prefer a small dinner reception; but the Contesse - that's the groom's mother - made a point of saying," she imitated the Contesse and illustrated her words by fluttering her fingers, "that she would be so thrilled to see her son waltz with his bride across a ballroom floor."

"'A' ballroom floor or 'the' ballroom floor?" asked a chambermaid.

"'A' ballroom floor," the cook replied.

"Let us pray it is not ours," the chambermaid added.

"Eat your breakfast and keep your remarks to yourself," the housekeeper said sternly.

It was evident that the staff did not like the Contesse. The cook, however, would not be intimidated. "That darling girl was ready to give her heart to Christ - but for Everett Junior's reckless driving, she'd be happy now in a place she knows and loves. And now that wretched woman is going to make her life miserable. She knows her foot's damaged, so she wants to see her waltz. Cruel, that's what it is. And don't tell me to be quiet. It isn't fair and that's the end of it."

There were no further comments during breakfast.

George returned to the hothouse and began to take an inventory of suitable white bridal flowers. His imagination went dead as he looked through the collection. He made a note to ask Sanford for suggestions the next time he saw him. He decided that his inability to be creative was due entirely to his preoccupation with the blonde young woman. He would cease being playful around her.

Beryl covered the nearly three hundred miles of the Commonwealth's width before she turned south and headed for Darmington, West Virginia.

She stopped at a gas station and café to refill and eat lunch. Following the directions the cashier had given her, she pulled up to the convent's gate at two o'clock, the precise time that the Prioress had agreed to meet her.

The Convent of Saint Catherine had once been a coal baron's mansion which was surrounded by a wall that made it ideal for conversion into a cloister. Beryl pulled on a bell-cord that dangled on the tall wooden gate and heard a tinkling sound in the distance. A moment later, a grated window in the gate opened, and the mouth and nose of a nun appeared. A small voice asked, "What do you want, please?"

"I have an appointment with Mother Angelica John. I'm Beryl Tilson from Philadelphia."

The gate slowly opened. Beryl entered and waited for the nun to close and lock it, so that she could follow her to the Prioress' office. They skirted the wall until they reached the level of the house, then they made a sharp turn and proceeded to the stone porch. She continued to follow the nun into the house, through the foyer, and all the way to the rear of the building. At the Prioress's office, the nun knocked and called, "Reverend Mother, the lady from Philadelphia is here."

"Show her in, Sister," a voice answered.

As Beryl entered, the prioress stood up. "Come along with me, Miss Tilson. We can talk while I attend to a problem in our workshop. Would you like to see what we manufacture here?"

"Yes, of course, Reverend Mother. I'd like that." She followed the prioress into the hall.

"You're interested in our little Lilyanne," the Prioress said, "but it is not our policy to discuss members of our order."

"I'm not trying to elicit information so much as I'm trying to verify information that has already been offered. Lilyanne Smith's future happiness may very well depend on these verifications."

"Your own eyes may answer your questions." She opened a door that led to a large workshop which had once, Beryl imagined, been the ballroom.

As the prioress talked to a supervising nun, Beryl watched working nuns, their sleeves pulled up and gartered, as they performed various tasks needed in the production of large wooden-bead rosaries. A few nuns, wearing protective goggles, stood at various machines. A drill cut a center hole into a long square shaft of wood. A lathe shaved and rounded it. A saw cut the shaft into half-inch length bead cylinders as nuns sat at grinding wheels and rounded the edges, before dropping the beads into a vat which smelled, Beryl thought, like linseed oil. Other nuns worked with metal, making links, and others, wearing welder's masks, soldered the links that attached the crucifix. At the end of the assembly line, a nun etched dedicatory passages, names, and dates into special gold crucifixes; and finally a group of nuns put finishing touches on all the rosaries and placed them into velvet-lined boxes.

Beryl asked, "Did Lilyanne work here?"

"Of course. Every nun works here."

"Which job did she do?"

"All of them. If you quote me, I will deny it; but the sad fact is that doing only one job, even if it is as spiritually rewarding as making rosaries, can get dreadfully boring. We therefore rotate through all of the tasks. All of them." She picked up two boxes that contained rosaries. "One for you and one for our dear Lilyanne."

Beryl thanked her as they walked back to the Prioress' office and sat down. Mother Angelica John folded her hands on her desk. "Is there anything else I can help you with?"

"I'd like to get a better fix on her as an individual," Beryl said. "What was her personality like?"

"Sweet. Innocent. Childlike in purity."

"And her physical health?"

"Once she had the flu. We all had it. We got through it with aspirin. We keep the usual antiseptics, vitamins and mineral supplements, Midol, pads, and Band Aids on the premises, as you'd expect. Nothing else."

Beryl hesitated before asking a question that seemed tangential to her line of inquiry. "For my own edification, Mother, could you tell me why Lilyanne selected your particular convent?"

The prioress shrugged. "I have no idea. It is never wise to ask since that generally entraps the postulant into lying about her motives." She smiled, "I'd be complicit in the sin."

Nodding an understanding, Beryl pressed on. "I know that in Zen Buddhism there was an ancient practice of the rich to donate a large sum of money to a monastery along with a young adult who was considered unmarriageable. Three birds were killed, so to speak, with that one stone. The young adult went from a state of shame to one of respect. The family was relieved of its embarrassing social burden, and the monastery could get its roof repaired. Is that what happened in her case?"

"The stone missed the first bird completely. The other two were sort-of on target."

"She didn't desire to go from shame to respect? Did she come here because she was spiritually drawn to the life?"

"Like no other postulant I have ever encountered. I would have said "nun" but as you know, she did not take her final vows."

"And 'sort-of' means...?"

"We definitely got the equivalent of a new roof. But the sort-of is that her father was probably not relieved to see her come here. He sent her gifts regularly. By gifts I mean a computer so that she could take online courses during her free time. When she took mathematics, he'd send the appropriate level of math books. When she wanted to learn a foreign language, she received CDs. For some courses, Astronomy, for example, he'd send DVDs and even a small telescope. While she did not have a formal college degree, she did get quite a comprehensive education. Being the sweet creature that she was, she'd make those gifts available for others to use."

"So she's - what's the term? an autodidact? Astronomy? I'm impressed. I took a college course once. I forget it all now. I don't know one constellation from another."

"I know the Big Dipper, and that's about it."

"One last question. Did anyone ever visit her or contact her in any way?"

"Our rule is no visitors except in emergency situations and for a few hours on two days, Christmas and Easter. Her father came to visit on those occasions. As to other communications, I have no way of knowing what letters the women send out; but I do see the letters that come in. Her father wrote to her regularly. I don't recall any other incoming mail for her. No one is permitted to send or to receive e-mail or to use a cellphone. And we have no public pay telephone on the premises."

As George slept in his apartment above the garage at Tarleton House, and Beryl slept in a Motel 6 on the Pennsylvania Turnpike, the four swindlers rested in their suite at The Declan Hotel in Philadelphia, having set in motion a scheme that would make them George Wagner's special quarry. He would soon make it his mission to bring them down, within or beyond lawful means. But on the fifteenth day of January, no mission had even been foreseen; and everyone slept peacefully.

SATURDAY, JANUARY 16, 2010

At The Declan, Charlotte lay upon the couch in one of the hotel's terrycloth bathrobes, pen and notepad in hand; her face covered in cream, her hair bound in a towel turban. She was making a "to do" list for the next "scene" in their production. Henri and Eric were watching television as the three of them waited for the fourth member of the 'cast,' Martin Shannon, to arrive.

Although Charlotte La Fontaine was indeed the Countess de Lisle and her son the legitimate heir to her late husband, she did not always play an aristocratic role in their "confidence" dramas. She could be a secretary, a corporate CEO, or a housekeeper. They were equals in the division of the spoils. Each was an accomplished actor, and none was weak enough to feel sympathy for a victim. Charlotte was the oldest member of the troop, and it was she who, drawing from an inexhaustible font of bitterness, nourished it and kept it strong.

At an age when other young women were preparing to attain majority, Charlotte Duran labored to be born anew. She had entered the world as another creature entirely in April, 1956, the youngest of seven children born into an upright middle class family in Montreal. Her parents dutifully sent their children to Catholic schools, attended Mass on Sundays, and obeyed all caste rules: the sons would go to college and the daughters would get married. No one anticipated the Women's Liberation Movement.

Charlotte, beautiful and far more intelligent than was beneficial to a woman of her social station, was encouraged by bra-burning rhetoric to create her own future. She intended to become a physician, a higher stratum routinely inaccessible to Catholic girls. At night, aside from insipid high school classes, she studied science and mathematics and passed the university's entrance examination with such high grades that she was offered a full academic scholarship.

Charlotte knew that the vanguard in any societal advance would struggle hardest. What she did not know was that the obstacles they encountered came less from the class they struggled to join than came from the class they struggled to leave.

Her three older sisters pleaded that it was unfair to give her an opportunity that had been denied them. Her brothers considered it a stupid waste of resources to deny a classroom position to a deserving young man and give it, instead, to a girl who was certain to marry, have children, and abandon the profession. Her father sought the advice of their parish priest who obliged by showing him illustrations from Grant's Anatomy and other texts and suggested that Charlotte, "who always was a little different" might be thought to have been motivated to touch a man's private parts and ogle photographs of diseased organs. "Was this something a girl from a respectable family would do?" he asked. Such sentiments were passed onto her mother who had "suspected as much."

Falsely pleading an inability to afford the cost of books, daily transportation, and other incidentals, her parents wrote to the university and declined the scholarship offer. They informed Charlotte of this correspondence at the dinner table. She would later recall, "My chest froze. I couldn't breathe. I saw their smirking faces and heard their contemptuous giggles. I could feel my body turn to ice, from the inside out. They hated me and I did not know why. Never have I felt such cold."

During the weeks that followed, she remained numb and lifeless. One day, in a bookstore she attracted the attention of a handsome man who was thirty-five years older than she. He was an impoverished French nobleman, Michel, le Conte deLisle, who was trying to verify a line in Baudelaire's *Fleur du Mal*. Seeing Charlotte and sensing her vulnerability, he returned Baudelaire to the shelf and removed a slim volume of Emily Dickinson's poems which he presented to Charlotte "as a bribe" he said, to have tea with him at a nearby tea shop. She accepted. For an hour he spoke gently to her, using the deferential terms accorded persons of rank, as she related the pain and disillusionment she had experienced when "a castle built in the air" had vanished in a cruel moment.

He showed her photographs of his once lovely but now dilapidated ancestral chateau, *Les Trois Cedres*, that was mortgaged along with its lands to the point of zero equity but which, unlike her castle, still stood on "terra firma." *Les Trois Cedres*, he explained, was in the beautiful Rhone-Alpes region of France, northeast of Lyon. He actually had been born in Martinique in a house that miraculously escaped the devastation of Mount Pelee's 1902 eruption, but which did not fare so well when Michel was nine years old, in Pelee's 1929 eruption. It currently was mostly buried in pumice, but enough of it had been excavated to make a part of the house habitable.

The intuition that would have made Charlotte an excellent physician informed her that he was sincere. He asked if she would like to be a countess in this nominally egalitarian age. She said she would. Did she understand that much money would be required to restore "their house and lands?" She said yes. Would she, as his wife, be willing to act as his partner in a less than orthodox way to gain the necessary funds? She nodded yes but asked for specifics. He said that he had a friend in The Hague who had a well-appointed residence in which many rich diplomats could be seduced, secretly videotaped, and then blackmailed.

He explained that she would need a new identity which meant costly documents, birth certificates, driver's license, and passport. They would also have to fly to Nevada where they could be married immediately. Would she be willing to get the necessary money by lending her body to a deserving gentleman? She said yes, and then she added, "But since I am a virgin, that must wait until after we spend our wedding night together and you teach me what to do to make the man's investment worthwhile."

The door to wealth and dignity and all that a man without conscience could ever hope to attain suddenly opened to Michel, le Conte deLisle. Astonished by her response, he took her hand, stood up, and then, kneeling on one knee before her in the tea shop, he kissed her hand. Charlotte's chest thawed, she drew a deep breath. She looked down at Michel La Fontaine and smiled with the pure mystery of a Madonna.

Immediately he changed the plan. "Under such a divine circumstance," he murmured, "I need only your photograph to send to The Hague. My friend will wire me the necessary funds to pay the document forger in Martinique. I would like you to have an old family name of mine for our wedding: Saint-Gilles. Will you become Charlotte Eleanor Saint-Gilles, a native born French citizen of Martinique whose address was Les Falaises, La Precheur, Martinique?" She nodded affirmatively.

When the documents were delivered to Michel, he made reservations for a Sunday afternoon flight to Nevada. Charlotte knew that unless she gave her family a reason for her departure, they might report her as missing. She therefore announced at the Sunday noon family dinner that she would be leaving home in a day or so since she had accepted a position with the archdiocese of New Orleans. "As what?" her father asked, and the others laughed at the absurdity of her statement. She waited for the laughter to subside, and then she softly answered, "I've been asked to work as an assistant to the head mistress of a convent school in the Bayou. The Peace Corps of France is working in the next Parish, but because the people speak Canadian or 'Cajun' French, we Quebecois are in demand. I'll be teaching elementary math and language." She prayed that he would remark about the change in climate or culture or even about the presence of alligators. He said nothing and continued to eat his dinner. The others ate and continued to make derisive comments, speaking about her in the third person. Her mother then made the mistake of saying, "Some man probably promised her that he'd make her a star in one of those dirty movies. She likes to look at dirty pictures."

Some insults that are made by friends or relatives can have an extraordinary effect upon a person. They are usually quiet little mockeries, as simple as a smirk shared with someone else that the person was not supposed to see, or a joking reference about a person's sex or love life that was supposed to be kept private. The insult, however slight it seems, is fatal.

To Charlotte, it was as if by a magical incantation her mother had brought to maturity a tiny creature that was gestating inside her. She stood breathless and silent as Charlotte Saint-Gilles filled the corpus that Charlotte Duran had occupied. The new essence percolated to the surface, squeezing the old one out of her pores. Instantly, she was of a different species, one that was no longer related to any of them. "For your information, I'm going now to meet the agent who hired me. She's leaving town this afternoon." She looked out the window. "Ah, it looks like rain. I ought to put my hair in a chignon." She hurried up the stairs to her bedroom which adjoined her parent's bedroom. While they laughed downstairs, she went into her mother's vanity and removed a long strand of large cultured pearls and earrings; a valuable 24 carat gold rosary; gold bracelets, broaches, necklace; a diamond dinner ring; and a diamond studded Longine wristwatch. From a tin box she stole the family's entire stash of money kept for emergencies and for her brothers' miscellaneous university expenses: twenty-four hundred dollars. She tucked her hair into the chignon and descended the stairs. "There's a chance I can get a ride this afternoon on the agent's chartered flight to New Orleans. If the nuns have room, I'll go and then send you a card or call in a few days. I don't need clothes. I'll be wearing a uniform. Otherwise, I'll be home for dinner."

She would never again set foot on Canadian soil, and she would never again squander empathy on anyone outside a privileged few. Rich and ruthless, she was, nevertheless, the young wife of an older man who was of retirement age when their only child was born. After twenty years of marriage, Michel died. It was necessary for Charlotte to form a small group of "like-minded souls" to acquire the large sums of money needed to provide for an aristocratic son and to maintain their divers dwellings.

This was the formidable woman who lounged on the couch at The Declan while Eric Haffner and her son Henri watched television. The two men, trim and nordic in appearance, were not difficult to tell apart. Henri had thick wavy hair and a schmisse, a fencing scar on his cheek. Eric's hair was straight and beginning to thin, letting his hairline recede, and he had no blemishes on his face. The lack of unusual features helped him to perfect the alterations in appearance he was often required to make.

Eric was a "remittance man," and, as such, received a reliable, though insufficient, income from his father's estate as payment for avoiding the continent of Europe. His family, bankers of integrity who fiercely guarded their reputation, would tolerate no misbehavior that could bring discredit upon them. Running against the family's grain, Eric was possessed of a lust for unusual forms of sexual gratification which he had not the slightest inclination to limit or to alter. He could easily meet the high academic standards his family imposed on him, but their ethical standards constituted a delightful source of amusement which, he thought, only a fool would seriously consider. At the age of thirteen he obtained instruction in meditation and seminal retention from an itinerant Tantric master. By sixteen he had mastered the techniques of "orgasm without ejaculation" and announced at dinner one evening that he had succeeded in becoming a tri-sexual. "I can enjoy males, females, and by the grace of God, myself." The news was not well received and doubt was cast upon his future in the banking industry.

His one friend at school was Henri La Fontaine. When the Haffners finally exiled him, the La Fontaines gave him citizenship. Until he acquired his own residence in the Cayman Islands, he considered *Les Falaises* (The Cliffs), then fully restored, to be his official residence. The only contact he maintained with his former family was through their accountants, and this, only to let them know where to send the next "remittance" check.

A room card-key was inserted into the door lock. The cast was now complete. Martin Williams Shannon, attired in a well-tailored chesterfield coat and bowler hat, entered and hung his coat in the closet before addressing anyone in the group.

"Love," he said to Henri, "do get me a whiskey and soda." Henri got up from the lounge chair and went to the bar to fix the drink.

"The Spruce Street place is perfect," Martin said between sips. "It's a corner property, with a high-fenced gated back yard for the pickup truck and limo. There are useable furniture pieces, a solid table and chairs in the kitchen, and fairly new but nondescript draperies."

"How much?" asked Charlotte.

"Two thousand for the month plus a thousand security deposit."

Eric looked up. "I drove past it yesterday. The location alone is worth three grand."

"When do we gain access?" asked Charlotte.

Martin took a key out of his pocket. "We already have it. I signed a 15th of January to 15th of February lease. I know that's cutting it close, but he had leased it to someone else, commencing February 16th. I'll start to set-up everything tomorrow."

"What reason did you give for wanting it for only a month?" Charlotte asked.

"I told the agent that my grandparents were having their golden wedding anniversary; and relatives were coming from all parts of the country." Martin swallowed hard to keep from laughing. "I inspected the roach infested upstairs bedrooms... I mean.... the wall paper was peeling off the walls and the place reeked of urine - I could barely inhale enough air to speak and tell him that they were perfect... just perfect!" He choked trying to restrain a burst of laughter. "I said that not all my relatives were prosperous. Some were missionaries who were vowed to poverty and gave every penny they had to their flocks." His laughter was infectious, and soon they all were rocking with laughter. "'Some,' I told him, 'were country parsons, poor as church mice but too pious to accept the gift of hotel accommodations.'" He began to laugh again and could barely speak the next sentence. "I confided that my generous brother was going to supply army cots and blankets and bring the food - macaroni salad, chitlins, okra, taco chips, and.. and," he put his head back and laughed merrily, "*guacamole dip.*"

Charlotte had tears in her eyes. "You're lucky that I don't have mascara on," she wheezed. "Ah... oh... You are such a joy." She sighed heavily and then began to laugh again.

When the laughter finally subsided, she said, "Well now, back to business. Do you have all the equipment you need to copy Wagner's keys?"

"Yes. I have the exact transponder keys and the Ford DIY guides and some equipment from a contact at the dealer. I shouldn't have any trouble with the remote keyless entry. He knows I'm not going to steal cars.

He offered to come with me, but I thanked him and gave him another $500 for his home phone number in case I do run into trouble. He gave me clear coding instructions. It's tricky to duplicate those transponder codes."

Martin Williams Shannon had been born in the Cayman Islands to Alice Williams, a cook, who married a mechanic named Shannon and moved to Jamaica where both were employed at a sugar plantation. When Shannon was killed in an accident caused by the owner's negligence, the family extended compensation by allowing five year old Martin, who had a calming effect upon their hyperactive son, to be included in the privately tutored classes at the plantation. The estate's *major domo* was British, the housekeeper was French, and the tutor was Portuguese. Martin, fluent in all three languages, obtained a college degree in business and acquired the manners and tony British diction that made him perfect as an estate manager and then, when that employment ended unhappily, as a swindler.

During the years he had managed the estate, he had sacrificed and saved, hoping to one day buy his own plantation. He kept his account in the same bank as his employers; but when the bank verged on failure, the bankers gave advance warning of its impending close to them and to a selection of friends which did not include Martin. He lost everything and when he protested that this "insider" information had been both unfair and illegal, he was dismissed from service.

For several years he was a beachcomber until the widow of a Haitian politician invited him onto her yacht and taught him the sexual techniques she had performed to convince a series of rich old men to marry her. Some of them had come by their wealth through a variety of fraudulent means, the methodologies of which she quickly learned. She also became expert in causing strife between her husbands and their children, sufficient to have the old men disinherit them.

In exchange for his sexual heroics, she became Martin's Scheherazade, delighting him nightly with an account of swindles, frauds, scams, cons, deceits, extortions, burglaries, spying, and blackmail - the complete catalog of schemes that she had acquired in her years of leisure. Furnished with an extensive gentleman's wardrobe and posing as the owner of a diamond rich *fazenda* near Quipelo, Angola, he escorted her to social events and acquired many casual friends among the rich and powerful. When her desire was diverted to a young Italian singer, she said goodbye to Martin, giving him as a parting favor a sloop named *Ingenue* she no longer wanted. Sailing had become his passion.

He never worked again unless it was in the cause of bilking strangers in order to maintain his new lifestyle. He fell in love with Charlotte the first time he saw her. Subsequently, he fell in love with Henri, too. When Michel died, he became one of the four members of Charlotte's newly formed "company."

"The Smith family," Martin observed, "should be good for at least three million in cash and jewelry."

Seeing Lilyanne peek at him from the vestibule of the hothouse, George, pretending to be busy, moved a few plants and began to sing "*A song of love is a sad song. Hi Lily, Hi Lily, Hi Lo…*"

Lilyanne giggled. "I knew you saw me…."

"You'd be difficult to miss. My nose would know. My nose can distinguish a Lily from all these orchids." His determination to be stolid had evaporated.

Lilyanne entered the hothouse and stood beside him. "When I was in the Convent, I missed these orchids so much. Some of them were like old friends. The blooms would last and last. Other flowers out on the grounds would bud and bloom and die. They'd last maybe a week. But the orchid flowers would bloom week after week. Sometimes the same flower would last for months! Honest! For months!"

"They just didn't want to leave you. As you said, they were your friends."

"What kind of flowers will you put on the reception tables? Did you hear? I'm supposed to get married. At least I think I'm supposed to get married."

"Who is the lucky young man?"

"His name is Henri. He's very handsome and charming - which I like, and he's also got a title which - I'll tell you in secret - my mother likes. Count or something. But he hasn't asked me yet. I don't know what to do."

"And you came to your old friends to tell them about it. Would you like me to work outside so you can have some privacy?"

"No, you sillybilly. I came to talk to you."

"Me? Ah, what did you want to talk to me about?"

"I saw you limp a couple of times. I limp, too. I wanted to ask you what happened to you."

"I used to be a policeman. I got shot in the knee and the shoulder. I had many surgeries too. "

"Ahh! You have scars, too? Can I see them?"

"I guess that will be all right. I only let special people see and since you are special…" He unbuttoned his shirt and bared his right shoulder.

"Did it hurt?" she asked.

"Not as much as yours."

"Oh. Yes. Mine did hurt. I put it all behind me. I have to look forward only."

"Are you looking forward to getting married?"

"No. I don't know how to be a wife. I have no social skills. I can't dance. I don't know how to meet people. I don't know how to dress. In the convent we ate so simply. Now I see dishes and I don't even know what they are much less how to eat them. I'll tell you something. I have never even been out on a date. I know I'm going to make so many mistakes."

George smiled. "One time I went into an Indian restaurant because I had spent time in a kind of ashram.. in California. I wanted to impress my date so I took her to this new Indian restaurant. It was a buffet style, but the little cards that identified the individual dishes were written in Sanskrit. We put lots of unrecognizable food on our plates and when it came to putting salad dressing on our salads, my date and I scooped rice pudding onto our salads. We went to our table to eat and a waiter came to tell us that we had put rice pudding on the salads. They have soupy rice pudding."

"What did you do?"

"Well, by the time the waiter came we had tasted some of the other food that was painfully hot and spicy. We couldn't eat it. He wanted to take our salad back and give us proper dressing, but we said, 'No! No! No, thank you. We prefer rice pudding on our salads.' Besides the bread, it was the only part of the dinner we could eat."

"I'll have to remember that when I make a mistake."

"That's right. Just act as if you intended to do whatever it was. Next thing other people will be imitating you. We had a lot of copycats in the restaurant that night."

She laughed. "You invented a new dressing, 'Rice Ranch.' Or did the chef name it after you?"

"I never went back to find out!"

She hooked her arm through his. "Do you have to stay here in the hothouse? Can you come out with me and walk through the grounds?"

"Sure. You can show me around."

They walked together down the brick pathways, talking about things to which time seemed to have added disproportionate value. She was thrilled to see an old elm tree. "I used to swing from this!" she cried. George shared her excitement. "Same thing for me!" he said. "I swung from an elm, too. We used an old tire." At the tennis courts she jumped up and down. "I was on my school team!" He told her that he used to play regularly and had gotten pretty good, too.

There were practice racquets and balls in a cabinet beside the courts. Laughing, they decided to play; but his right arm was so weakened by his shoulder injury that when he served, the ball barely went over the net. She, too, had so much trouble running forward to hit what amounted to a series of drop shots, that she missed the ball entirely. "I think we need a little work," George said. Laughing, they returned the balls and racquets to the cabinet. She sighed, "I will say a prayer tonight that Henri doesn't like to play tennis."

"With practice you'll get better," George said.

"Unfortunately, the swimming pool is covered," Lilyanne noted with a grin.

"Oh, I don't know," he replied. "I bet we used to be good at ice skating."

"I was!" she shouted. "I really was." Again they laughed.

Suddenly George grew sad. "I don't want you to catch cold," he said, steering her towards the big house.

"I had so much fun, today. Thank you, Mr. Wagner."

"Tennis partners use their first names. Call me George."

She giggled and ran into the house.

Sensei was sitting in the office when Beryl returned from visiting the convent. "How was the trip?" he asked.

Beryl flopped into her desk chair. "Great. I stayed overnight in a motel and had a really good night's sleep. Perfect weather on the turnpike."

"And the interview? Was it successful?"

"Completely. They make wooden rosaries, mostly for priests… and they make them from scratch. The nuns rotate through all the jobs. She did everything: operate a lathe, weld, engrave on gold."

"George asked a friend of his to check with The Declan. He called back and said that there were four people registered in the suite." Sensei picked up a telephone message pad and read, "Three bedroom suite. Charlotte La Fontaine, a.k.a. the Contesse deLisle, and her son, Henri, had two of the bedrooms, and two servants occupied the third bedroom: Eric Haffner, the chauffeur, and a big black guy with a Jamaican passport, Martin Shannon, who is Henri's valet. The Contesse's credit is good. No problems whatsoever. I had her credit rating checked, and she's solid, financially."

"I think I'll be missing services tonight. All that driving and I'd like to soak in the tub."

"Well, I gotta go open the temple. Pronto." Sensei went out the front door, checked it to see that it had locked behind him, and hurried down Germantown Avenue to his small Zen temple half a block away.

George went to the pub again on Saturday night. Someone called, "Are you up for a game?" "Sure," he answered, and brought his bottle of beer to the shuffleboard. It was a close game, but George and his teammate won. The atmosphere was convivial when they retreated to the bar.

Pete revealed that he worked for the contractor who installed the watering system in the Tarleton hothouse. "How is it working out?" he asked.

"Great. It's a fantastic piece of work," said George. "State of the art!"

Between games, George hazarded a question about the Smith's late, wayward son. The plumber filled him in for twenty minutes on some of the boy's escapades. "If he hadn't wrapped his sportscar around that tree, he would've died at the hands of one of us. The Smiths let him get away with murder. They didn't give a shit about his little sister. He was the star. Good lookin'. Athletic. Girls always chasing him. We thought he was a stupid fuck. He'd drive down the streets doin' 80. Kids, cats, dogs, he didn't give a shit. Everybody had to get out of his way."

"Why didn't they care about the girl?" George asked.

"She was too independent. They said she was 'backward.' But she went to a private bording school with other rich girls so she had to be smart. They're the stupid ones. They had a big barbecue accident with lighter fluid. She tried to prevent the accident and they blamed her for causing it. She got badly burned. After that she got real religious. They couldn't get her into a convent fast enough. As soon as she was eighteen, off she went. Jesus… that was about five years ago."

George noticed that his breathing rate had changed. He was feeling angry and frustrated. Pete continued, "And then their precious son got his brains smeared all over a windshield and they brought her back - to breed her like a sow."

George managed to fake a laugh. "Who understands the rich?" he said, his mouth going dry. He didn't know why, but he needed to get out of the pub. He thanked Pete for the good game and the good conversation and said he hoped to see him again soon. "We'll beat the shit out of all comers."

"Right on," said Pete.

SUNDAY JANUARY 17, 2010

Even after he took his evening medication George had spent a restless night in his little apartment over the garage. An overhead light outside the garage was kept on all night; and though he stared at the light continuously, his eyes did not want to tire and close from the strain. He would drift into sleep but then he would awaken thinking about everything that went wrong in his life, starting with the night that he walked into an ambush.

At 8 a.m. he called the kitchen and asked if a breakfast tray could be brought up to him, with an extra cup of coffee.

Jane, the kitchen maid, carried the tray to him. "Out having a good time last night?" she asked.

"I guess… if you consider playing shuffleboard a good time."

She raised her eyebrows. "I don't even know what that is."

"If you've ever been in a bar and there was a long skinny table and people at each end sliding pucks back and forth… that's shuffleboard."

"I wondered what those tables were for," she said cheerfully. "If you want more coffee, just ring the kitchen. I'll bring you a whole pot if you want."

He thanked her. "What do I do with the breakfast tray?"

"Just bring it back to the kitchen whenever you can. There's not much routine today. Everybody's gone to church. Then the family is supposed to go from church to some relatives for brunch. We don't expect them back until mid-afternoon."

She left. George finished eating, but didn't drink his coffee. Instead, he went back to bed and this time he slept soundly.

At 3 p.m. as he was mixing orchid food, Lilyanne came to the hothouse. Her eyes were red, he noticed, as she said, "Hello Tennis Partner George."

"Hello. You look as if you've been crying. It's not the time of year for allergies."

"Well... to tell you the truth, my mother is worried about my limping down the aisle. She says it will embarrass her and daddy."

"Come over here," he said, indicating an area over which a lead pipe ran. "I'm going to lift you up until you can hold onto the pipe with both hands and just relax and hang there. I want to see if your toes are the same length. Is that ok with you?"

"Sure," she said. He lifted her and let her hold on to the pipe. Then he removed her shoes and pressed her stockinged feet together.

"They're both the same length," he said, "so an insole lift isn't going to help. Does it hurt you when you step down on your foot?" He clasped her waist and lowered her.

She slipped on her shoes. "No, but I always remember how it used to hurt and I just got into the lazy habit of favoring that foot."

"Then," he said, "that's what we have to work on. No more lazy foot!" He took her by the arm and gently guided her to a stairway that led down to a gazebo. "You hold onto the railing," he said, "and I'll go down and watch you. First one foot on one step, and then the other foot on the next step. No stopping with both feet on the same step."

Awkwardly she tried to descend the stairs without letting her feet rest together. It was difficult, but she did it. He made her go up the steps the same way.

They practiced for fifteen minutes and returned to the hothouse. She promised that she would practice in the big house. "Do you think I'll be able to do it by Wednesday night?"

"What happens Wednesday night?"

"Henri and his mom are coming to dinner. I think he's going to give me an engagement ring. Sanford will be telling you what kind of centerpiece to make. Mama hasn't picked the table linens yet."

"Soon you will be an old married lady."

"No! Not old!"

"Then a beautiful young married lady."

"I'll be going shopping tomorrow to buy a new dress for dinner and also a gown and wrap for the opera Monday night. And I think Henri is going to take me out on Friday night. So maybe I'll be getting three new dresses. I'll find out Wednesday night what kind of dress I need for the Friday night date. We'll be going to the bank vault to get some of mama's jewelry for me to wear. I think he's going to give me an emerald ring so I'll be getting lots of her emerald stuff. We just had brunch with my cousin, Felice. She's going to be my maid of honor and she and her husband are going to the opera with us. They'll be coming to dinner Wednesday night, too."

"You are going to be so busy!" George suddenly saw Sanford walking towards the hothouse. "Here comes Sanford. I guess he's going to give me instructions."

A particularly beautiful white orchid was sitting back far enough from the aisle to avoid accidental contact. "That," George said, pointing at it, "is called *Lycaste virginalis-alba*, the national flower of Guatemala, the exquisite *Monja Blanca*, the White Nun." He picked up a scissors, reached over other plants, and cut the single flower, keeping its stem as long as possible. "Here," he said, "the rare and beautiful for the rare and beautiful."

"Ahh! George! Mama loves that orchid."

"And now it is just a pretty decoration," he inserted the flower into her hair above her left ear, "for your pretty face."

Sanford had entered the hothouse. He looked at Lilyanne. "Hmm," he said. "It's beautiful in your hair."

"I mean it, George, my mother will be furious. Suppose she fires you. It's the only one we have."

"That is why I cut it," said George. "Did you ever hear the Zen story about the morning glories?" Sanford paused to listen.

"When morning glory plants first came to Japan, they were all the rage; but only a few people had them. One Zen master gained instant fame for the beautiful morning glories he grew all around the fences of his tea room. So another master wrote to him, saying that he would be in town on the following Thursday. Could he come by for morning tea and see the flowers? The Zen master wrote back and said he would expect him Friday morning. When Friday came the Zen master went around the tea room and cut off every morning glory but one... the one that he thought was the most beautiful one. And this one he put into a vase and set it inside the tea room for the visiting master."

Lilyanne smiled. She understood. Sanford looked puzzled. "Why did he cut all the others down?"

Lilyanne grinned. "It was a version of the law of supply and demand. The one morning glory became so much more precious because it was one of a kind."

"Oh, I get it. But your mother won't. If she sees it in your hair, she'll be very angry. So I think this is what we should do. I'll get a glass of water and put a few drops of freshening liquid in it. You can keep it here in a secret place," he looked around, "and you can put it in your hair whenever you visit the hothouse or whenever your mother is not at home."

"Problem solved," said George.

"I wish I could see how it looks."

"I'll bring a mirror from the house as soon as I finish with Wagner," Sanford said.

Later, when Sanford returned with the mirror, he told them that sandwiches would be served in the kitchen for the rest of the day. "Open board," he called. "Mr. and Mrs. Smith are out and will be out for the evening, playing bridge with friends."

"Tell George how I've been practicing."

"She has. There is not a staircase at Tarleton that she has not gone up and down without putting both feet on the same step. Very stylish. Very graceful."

"But I'm such a neanderthal. I've never had a date and I don't know how to dance. I'm so scared that I'm going to make a fool of myself. Mama will be so embarrassed."

George went into the vestibule and took a radio off the shelf. "Here," he plugged it in, "let's have a dance lesson."

Sanford moved a wheelbarrow and some tools out of a corner of the hothouse. "Your ballroom floor, *Mademoiselle*."

George found a station that was playing "Oldies but Goodies" dance music. Julie London was crying a river. "Ok," he said, "you have to remember 'Quick-quick-slow.' Can you remember that?"

She nodded. They awkwardly began the dance, but after a few bars, she was able to keep the beat.

They completed the dance. She hugged him and laughed jubilantly. "But," she said sadly, "I still don't know about having a date."

"I'll tell you what," said George. "Since your parents are going out tonight, let me come and call for you for a formal date. I'll come to the house to take you to the ball. We won't get farther than the portico, but at least you'll be experienced at being called for on a date."

Lilyanne giggled. "My first date! And what time will you call for me?"

"I shall call for you at six thirty."

George prepared for his date. In the garage he had seen two fox tails that had been fixed to the handle bars of a bicycle. He pinned the tails to the back of a gardener's smock, made a corsage of a spray of phalenopsis flowers, and wrote a name on a small piece of cardboard.

It was dark as he walked up to the main house and knocked on the front door. Sanford answered, and said, "Yessss?"

George handed him the card. Sanford read it and called, "Sir Pent Fer deLance is calling for Miss Lilyanne."

Wearing a long bathrobe, Lilyanne stood at the top of the curving staircase which led into the foyer. George and Sanford watched her slowly descend one step after the other without putting both feet on the same step. As she reached the bottom, Sanford and George applauded. George pinned the corsage to her bathrobe. The cook and the kitchen maid came to see what was happening.

"Oh, Sir Pent!" Lilyanne giggled, "you're wearing your tails!" Everyone laughed as George gallantly offered her his arm. Sanford opened the door with a flourish and the daters stepped over the threshold.

Outside, George paused, bowed, and said, "Thank you for a lovely evening, Miss Lilyanne. May I telephone you next week?"

"Please do, Sir Pent," she said. "I shall look forward to receiving your call. Good night."

Everyone applauded. George returned to his apartment, gathered his laundry, and went to the hothouse to set the watering timers and lock the building. Then he went to his pickup truck and drove all the way to his office. He wanted to attend the Sunday night services at the little Zen Temple down the street from his office. He needed spiritual guidance.

As he approached the building he could smell the sandalwood incense and hear the muffled sounds of chanting. It was the Heart Sutra. He began to chant softly with the others as he entered. He took his seiza bench and mat from the rear storage area and, still chanting, quietly placed them in the aisle between the wall and Beryl's mat. He liked to listen to the ticking clock that Beryl, who functioned as the bell-ringing time keeper, used to measure the segments of the service. The chant ended. She picked up a little bell and rang it. It was the 8:45 signal for Sensei to begin his Dharma talk.

"The principles of ethical behavior," Sensei began. George heard nothing else until Sensei reached the final section of his talk. "The eye cannot see itself!" Sensei asserted. "The Buddha reminds us: 'A man broadcasts the faults of others like winnowing chaff in the wind, but hides his own faults as a crafty fowler covers himself.'"

Sensei continued, "And so we tend to become like duck hunters. We cover ourselves with brambles to make us appear like a good place for ducks to take shelter or nest. We put painted wooden birds in the water to attract them as they fly by, tempting them to approach. But when those birds accept our invitation and descend, we shoot them. We reveal our true motives. The birds come to the pond and discover, too late, that they could never mate with wooden birds and there was no safety in those brambles."

George cringed thinking about his ridiculous barking episode and the fox tails, pretending to be playing with a young bride-to-be as though she were his daughter. And then the tennis and the dancing. "What the hell was I thinking?" he asked himself. The answer was simple: he was trying to endear himself to the girl. Charm her like a duck hunter with decoys. And to what end?

He did not hear the next few minutes of the talk. His mind was reviewing the day's events and trying to find an acceptable reason for giving those idiotic dance lessons. If only he hadn't held her in his arms… lifted her.. danced with her. Something magnetic had happened to him. He had touched a live wire. "What the hell was I thinking?" He began to listen again.

Sensei concluded his Dharma talk. "Can self-blindness be overcome? Yes, by holding a mirror up to ourselves and knowing that by so doing, we are daring to look at Medusa's face. What we see is often fatal to our self-esteem. This is the reason that we say that Zen is a cauldron of boiling oil over a roaring fire. We must be cautious! It can be dangerous to see our own truth."

Beryl rang the chimes and Sensei called out the name of the next chant.

George mumbled the chant by rote. He was thinking. It seemed to him to be some kind of cruel coincidence that Sanford had brought a mirror to the hothouse. "The eye cannot see itself," he muttered. He would have to look in that hothouse mirror and see what it was he saw.

MONDAY, JANUARY 18, 2010

Monday morning George came directly to the office and told Beryl about the events at the pub and the hothouse.

Beryl laughed. "You? You with all the flexibility of a mummy... you gave her dancing lessons?"

"Yes, and I was good. In the land of the lame and inexperienced, the man who has one good leg and used to know his way around a dance floor is Fred Astaire. Sanford took a few steps with her, too. I was better."

"So you found your Ginger Rogers?"

"No, I retired from the stage. No more rosin and grease-paint. Let's get the case written up."

They sat together and item by item listed the intention and the result of each action they had taken thus far in the investigation. They assembled all the receipts and created another sheet to itemize expenses.

At The Declan, Charlotte sat on the couch, trying on rings. "I don't want to outshine your engagement ring," she said to Henri. "I think I'll wear sapphires. And my blue Valentino with my white fox."

Henri, lounging on the couch, agreed. "Did you make an appointment with the hairdresser?"

"Yes. Wednesday at 2 p.m.." She put the sapphire ring in the box and closed it. "I can't wait until we're back in the Caymans or Martinique. This weather is vile."

"I think I'll buy a new schooner," Martin said, tussling Henri's hair. "Two masts."

"Whatever you want, " Henri stretched.

Charlotte examined her toes. "I suppose Eric will spend a few days with me at my house?"

Eric made himself a drink. "Maybe a couple of weeks. After we split up the money I think I'll buy another place farther inland. I'm tired of all that ocean. I'd like to see nothing but green hills and trees and flowers. I heard about an abandoned mining operation. They built a first class house and assay lab for the manager. Come with me to check it out. Twenty acres come with it." He sat at Charlotte's feet. "Rub my shoulders."

"First let me call the executive airport to make sure the mechanics have finished the Piper's tune up." She took a disposable cellphone from her purse and called the airport. Charlotte had been a licensed pilot since Michel had purchased a Piper Dakota for her when she was pregnant with Henri. She flew the plane frequently in her alternate identity as a citizen of Suriname. The plane, she was told, was ready to go.

Eric stretched and yawned. "I'd like to spend time in Martinique. This is the Caribbean dry season. When it's all over in the Caymans, let's go to *Les Falaises* so I can have another session with that girl who sells vegetables on the boat. The bitch scratched me. I think the marks are permanent." He pulled off his T-shirt. "Can you see them?"

"No," Charlotte said, scrutinizing the flesh on his back. "You have the hide of an elephant." She began to massage his shoulders.

WEDNESDAY JANUARY 20, 2010

George arrived at Tarleton House at 7 a.m. He went directly to his apartment, unpacked his clothing and put his toiletries and medicines in the bathroom. He watched the morning news for half an hour and then went to the main house for breakfast with the staff.

Sanford called him aside. "Madam would like to know if you'd do her the favor of staying here for the night. There will be a celebration tonight and some of the guests will be staying overnight. We'll therefore have breakfast for five - I doubt that the cousins will stay overnight, but it's possible since the weather is supposed to turn bad - and she'd like a fresh arrangement as a centerpiece. She'll use white linens so any color will do. She'll likely use the closed patio. And, would it be possible if their chauffeur stayed in your quarters? Madam doesn't like chauffeurs to stay inside the house. They tend to come and go at all hours."

George agreed to the accommodation. Sanford nodded and instructed the staff maintenance man to take the rollaway bed to George's room. He also told the new maid to put extra blankets on the cot and to give Mr. Wagner extra blankets, too.

Lilyanne had gone to the beauty parlor to have her hair styled in a kind of tamed Gibson Girl bouffant arrangement that complemented her high lace-collar beige silk gown.

In the evening, George stood hidden in a group of spruce trees near the entrance of Tarleton House and watched Henri and the Contesse arrive in the limousine. He watched as Eric opened the rear door and stood at attention while Henri, in formal evening attire, exited the car and bent forward, extending his hand to help his mother. Charlotte, her ear lobes and neck sparkling with diamonds, carried herself regally as she mounted the stone steps, her hand resting on the upraised hand of her son.

Just as George started to return to the garage apartment he saw another car's headlights approach. This would be James and Felice Barton, Lilyanne's cousin and her husband.

Instead of returning to his apartment, George went to the rear of the house and went downstairs to the kitchen. "Is there anything I can help with?" he asked the cook.

"No," Letty answered. "But if you want to see how beautiful Miss Lilyanne looks - this was her very first time in a beauty parlor getting her hair styled - she was so excited - so if you want to sneak a look, go upstairs by the servants' staircase… it's enclosed and dark so take a flashlight. You'll see a door there with a grated window in it. That one opens into the dining room. Keep walking and you come to another door. That one opens into the parlor. That's where they all are now. Make sure your flashlight doesn't shine into the glass."

Had Lilyanne been a suspect in a crime, George would have had no reluctance to peek at her; but she was not a suspect; and he hesitated to go up and see her since his motive arose from more than idle curiosity. That the cook so clearly recognized his desire to see her, embarrassed him. He momentarily debated with himself, but then Letty commanded, "Go on! Go on, while they're still in the parlor." He took one of the flashlights she kept near the base of the staircase and went up to look. He did not recognize Lilyanne, believing for a moment that she was her cousin. But then he saw her dark haired cousin, Felice, and as his eyes returned to Lilyanne, his knees grew weak. He backed away from the window and slumped against the wall. Slowly, he stood up straight, returned to the staircase, and descended to the kitchen. "I need my head examined," he muttered to himself disgustedly.

He thanked the cook for her help and said, as casually as he could manage, that "she sure looks good. They all do. Quite a gathering." As he opened the kitchen door to leave, he called to the cook, "I'll be in the apartment over the garage. If you need me for anything at all, just ring."

Letty shouted after him, "Save some room for the engagement cake. I'm sure there'll be plenty left over. We'll be sending you a piece."

"Fine," he answered, turning around to wave.

He called Beryl to learn about the results of her investigations into the Smith family fortune. "They are the genuine article," she said. "Sensei also asked a few of his friends for the lowdown on the family, and evidently while they may not be the nicest folks on the block, they were certainly the most 'responsibly rich' he was told. So unless you find any bodies buried in the basement or the petunia patch, the Contesse has nothing to worry about. More to the point," Beryl added, "tell me what everyone wore."

George had no sense of fashion and could barely describe in intelligible terms the gowns the four women had worn to the party.

They gossiped about things of minor importance, the rollaway bed that was now on the other side of his bedside table and the extra blankets for the cold, and then, since Beryl wanted to soak in the tub, the conversation ended and he turned on the Tv.

At nine o'clock Letty called from the kitchen. "Are you ready for that cake? Miss Lilyanne would like each one of the staff to celebrate the happy occasion with her and have some cake and champagne. Their chauffeur is going to bring it over now."

"Can I pass on the champagne and just have milk?"

"Yes, you can," she said. "I'll make sure you get a nice piece, and Eric will get one too. He'll be there in a minute."

Eric had seen George the day he delivered the Contesse to the investigator's office. He stood outside the apartment door and called, "Wagner, it's me, Eric. Can you open the door? I've got my hands full with my overnight bag and the tray."

The two men sat on their beds and ate the cake with the milk. George asked, "What did her engagement ring look like?" and Eric shrugged. "How should I know? I'm just the chauffeur. They don't do 'show and tell' for me." At this exchange, they both laughed. George began to feel sleepy. "I hope they don't need me for anything. I'm really crashing." Eric said, "Me, too. Sugar is a soporific. People think it perks a person up to eat sugar. It doesn't. The chocolate might if it has a lot of caffeine in it. My doctor in London told me that milk and cookies is a great bedtime snack providing the cookies are not chocolate." George barely heard this last sentence.

Fifteen minutes later, Eric got George's keys and made impressions of the house and office keys. Then he heard a light tap on the door and he went outside and handed the molds, the pickup's keys, and the ring of office and house keys to Martin Shannon who was carrying a large case.

Martin took the key to the pick-up, opened the door and climbed in. He opened the case and, using a battery operated laser key grinding machine, made a duplicate of the transponder key. He inserted the key into the ignition, then using a computer that was programmed to access the truck's anti-theft digital coding system, he transferred the code to the new transponder key. He made new keyless entry remotes. He tested both sets of keys and entry remotes several times, and, satisfied that they worked, he checked to see that he had all the blanks he needed to make copies of George's home and office keys. He had all the blanks for these standard locks and quickly ground copies of them.

Martin put the duplicate of George's ignition key and the back-up clay impressions Eric had made in his carrying case. He packed his equipment, and making sure he had left no prints or grinding dust behind, he got out of the truck, locked it, retested the opener, locked it again, and returned the keys to Eric. Then he walked to the rear of the estate and, using a flashlight, followed a narrow path that led through a wooded area to the chain link fence in which he had cut an opening. He squeezed through the opening, picked up the bolt cutters he had used and left hidden in some nearby brush, and walked to his small rented car.

Eric had meanwhile opened George's night time prescription bottle to see whether the capsules could be opened and were big enough to hold a sufficient amount of the sedative he had put in George's milk.

He took a tranquilizer from his own bottle of pills, turned off the television, undressed, got into the cot and went to sleep.

THURSDAY. JANUARY 21, 2010

At 7 a.m., Eric left the room while George slept. At the main house he had breakfast with the staff and then he lingered in the kitchen until Henri summoned him at nine o'clock. Eric, Henri, and the countess left the estate grounds and headed back to The Declan.

Eric parked the limo and went with the others to the suite. He changed his clothes and took the keys to the rented Ford sedan and a manila envelope that contained some folded paper bags and began the long drive to Princeton, New Jersey. He had to mail the envelope to Henri at The Declan.

George slept until ten. Feeling unusually dull, he took a cold shower. As he walked to the hothouse, he saw that the limousine and the Barton's BMW were gone.

After he checked to see that everything was in order in the hothouse, he went to the main house kitchen. "I expected to see a horde of society page reporters around the house…. maybe a few helicopters," he said as he sat down at the staff's dining table.

"The Contesse," said Sanford, "thought that since the wedding was going to be so intimate and that the reception would be given at Tarleton, 'around which there was no moat,' as she put it, it would probably be best to limit the news now but to have an enormous reception when the honeymooners returned. She would give that reception in New York, at the Hotel Pierre - if that would be acceptable to the Smiths - which, of course, it was. She said that this would establish a balance and Henri's relatives and friends from Europe would also feel included in the grand event."

"Did you see her ring?" George asked.

"Yes," Sanford answered proudly. "It looked to me to be three carats of emerald surrounded by diamonds. Quite beautiful."

The cook laid out an assortment of foods left over from the evening's dinner; but while the rest of the staff lined up and filled their plates, George only drank tea. Then he thanked the cook and headed for the hothouse. The case was over. The staff had been nice to him and he regretted that they soon would know that he had been there as a spy of sorts. He knew that Lilyanne fascinated him and this, alone, would make it impossible for him to consider remaining on the job. But this, he decided, he would keep to himself.

He began to organize the potting supplies and to enter new invoices into the journal.

"George," Lilyanne called softly. "Oh, George."

He looked up to see her peeking at him from just outside the vestibule. "Well, Hello, Soon-to-be-Lady Lilyanne."

She laughed. "That sounds so funny. I came to show you my ring and to ask a favor of you."

She held out her hand and he blinked at the beauty of the ring. "Wow!" he said. "That is one beautiful ring! And what is the favor you want of me?"

"I want you to teach me something."

"Sure."

"Next Monday night we're going to the opera to see *Gotterdammerung*. Felice, James, Henri and *moi*. I got a new gown and wrap to wear. You should see it. It's green velvet and I'll be wearing all my mom's really nice jewelry… diamond and emerald tiara… earrings… necklace… bracelet… and my beautiful ring. I never thought I'd see the day that she'd put that tiara on my head. My father gave it to her for their tenth wedding anniversary."

"But what is the favor you want of me?"

"George… Tell me how I should act at the opera. I've never been to one."

George stood up and sat on the edge of his desk. "Let's see… your mom should have opera glasses. Ask her if you can borrow them. Henri will come here to pick you up, and you'll go to the opera house and climb the steps and go to… probably a box… some special seats… like your own private section. If not, then you'll have good seats downstairs. And you know how when you see a foreign film you see the English captions down at the bottom, well in an opera the English captions are above the stage. That's the only difference. It's a long opera so there are usually two intermissions. You'll go out into the lobby or a special area on the box level, the mezzanine, and get champagne and sometimes *hors d'oeuvres*. You should pass on the *hors d'oeuvres* because you'll probably have long gloves on and what's the point? Sometimes they are loaded with garlic. And that's all there is to it."

"I'm still scared."

"Will you be wanting a corsage for your date Friday night?"

"No," she said. "Henri got a call just before we had dinner last night. He has to go to New York to sign some papers for his uncle. So I won't be seeing him again until Monday night when we go to the opera."

He watched her walk spiritedly back towards the main house; and then he called The Declan and asked to be connected to the suite of the Contesse deLisle.

Martin answered the call and after checking to see if "Madame is available," transferred the call to Charlotte who sounded sleepy. "Ah, do forgive me" she said, "I was napping."

George apologized for disturbing her. "I think we can safely say that the case is concluded - and in a favorable way. That's refreshing to a P.I. It usually doesn't work out so well."

Charlotte protested. "But you are not finished! I have my doubts about the girl. She had a glass of champagne last night and she was positively giddy. She didn't speak much but what she said often didn't make sense or was inappropriate. It disturbed Henri, and, I must say, it disturbed me. She certainly is pretty enough… though I cannot imagine her lying on the beach at St. Tropez. But her social presence is far from adequate. She's awkward and her shyness is becoming a little annoying.

'Still water runs deep.' And what about her family? Are they a lot of show or are they substantial?"

George assured her that they had found nothing to suggest that the Smith family of Tarleton House was anything less than financially sound. "Their wealth is substantial. All of the checks we ran indicated that they are what you were led to believe. Both parents come from families that have been rich for generations."

"Very well. I trust your integrity as investigators. Submit your report to me regarding your findings on the Smith's financial soundness. But I insist that you cannot possibly have investigated her fully. She is the type that naturally engenders sympathy. Just before Henri left to attend to some business in New York, he received a call from a friend of his who knows the Smith family. He said that he had heard the girl was mentally or morally defective. I wanted details, but Henri was so furious with his friend for repeating such gossip that he immediately cut off their conversation. I must be reassured that it *is* gossip. What in the world would my family think if I were warned about this possibility and chose to ignore the warning? I'd like you to continue on the job. If you've used up the twenty thousand dollars, I will give you more. Submit what you've done so far, but please continue until she has made her first public appearance with my son on Monday evening, the twenty-fifth. We simply must be sure."

He wanted to put an end to the case. "Well," he said slowly, "I can't leave these people high and dry when it comes to the hothouse. All right. We can make next Monday night at midnight the endpoint. I mean… there has to be a cut-off."

Charlotte thought for a moment. "Fine. But I would still like to look over the reports of what you've already learned. Would you personally drop them off at the desk at The Declan tomorrow morning? Make sure they are in a well sealed envelope and that they are specifically addressed to me. And be sure your business name and address are not on the envelope."

George agreed to hand deliver the reports to the desk clerk in the morning. He thought the countess's caution excessive, but he agreed to continue to observe Lilyanne.

He called Beryl and told her to prepare an interim report of her investigations and expenses. "We won't officially be finished until Monday night, but the Countess wants a report as of five o'clock today. I hadn't planned to come to the office after work, but I have to now, to get my own stuff ready. So let's bring everything we've got and go over it at dinner. Bring your laptop. I'll be so goddamned glad to get this case over with."

"It hasn't been that bad," she answered. "But you sound so... I don't know... defeated."

"It's getting to be too stressful. Christ! For ten years it's been one thing after another. I keep thinking I've reached the limit, but then the goddamned boundary moves."

FRIDAY, JANUARY 22, 2010

After George dropped off the report at the hotel desk early Friday morning, he went to the hothouse and prepared for the emotional drag the weekend promised. Wanting to be anywhere but there, he found reasons to go shopping for new soils and fertilizers and to drive out to Haddonfield to a wholesale orchid breeder to purchase several Monja Blanca plants, one of which he bought for himself. When he returned to the hothouse and dropped off the supplies, he planned to go out for a sandwich and then to play shuffleboard at the Pub.

At 4:30 p.m. as George was still driving back from Haddonfield, Eric Haffner parked his rented sedan a block from the Pub and opened his disguise kit. He removed a shoulder-length, straggly blonde wig and inserted a theatrical denture into his mouth. He studied himself in the rear-view mirror, and satisfied that his wig looked natural, he removed a flask of bourbon from the kit, took a swig, swished it around his mouth and swallowed it. He drove to the pub and pulled into the parking lot.

Appearing like a man who had been drinking but was far from drunk, he put his foot on the brass rail and leaned on the bar.

"What'll you have?" the bartender asked.

"Gimme' a Heineken."

As the bartender nodded affirmatively and turned away to get the beer, Eric laid a twenty dollar bill on the bar and called, "Has George been in yet?"

"George who?" the bartender replied as he opened the bottle and set it on the bar. He picked up the bill to ring up the sale. A few patrons at the bar began to listen.

"George Wagner, the P.I. who's workin' up at Tarleton." He began to guzzle the beer.

"P.I.? Good lookin' guy with a bum hand?" He laid the change on the bar.

"Yeah," said Eric. "Takes care of the hothouse. I was supposed to meet him here. But I may have gotten the time wrong." He feigned a look of befuddlement. "I could swear he said 4:30 p.m."

"The few times he came in here, it was more like 7 or 8. So he's a private investigator?" He grew defensive. "What the hell did he expect to find in here that needs investigating?"

Eric drained the bottle and looked at his watch. "Gimme another," he said, "and he wasn't lookin' for anything here." He burped. "It was the owners of the place, Tarleton… something.."

"The Smiths? What's goin' on in their hothouse? Are they growing weed or funny mushrooms?" Several patrons overheard the remark and laughed as the bartender took the empty bottle away and returned with a new one.

"Nuthin' so exciting. Their kid is marrying a duke or a prince, and his family is making sure they're legit." Eric picked up the bottle.

The bartender shrugged. "All I know is that he works there in the hothouse with their orchids. How that's supposed to help him investigate the Smiths, I don't know." He took money from the bar and rang up the sale.

"Hey… neither do I. Flowers are his hobby. He's an ex-cop… a P.I. pro." Eric drank half of the bottle. "I was supposed to do a little job for him. Damn! I'm sure he said Friday. But he also talked about some work on Monday night. Shit. It's after six now. Well, he knows where to reach me." He finished the beer and placed the bottle on the bar and picked up most of his change. "If he comes in lookin' for Harry, do me a favor and tell him to call me."

"Sure," said the bartender. "Will do."

As soon as Eric left the pub, one of the patrons said, "That guy who played shuffleboard with Pete is actually an investigator? That's news."

At 5 p.m., as George was unloading the supplies, the hothouse phone rang. Sensei, who was concerned about George's uneasy mood, called to ask George to come to services and then to go out - the way they used to - to play shuffleboard. George agreed, but stipulated, "I'll play shuffleboard but I want it understood that there'll be no talk about this goddamned job I'm on."

SATURDAY, JANUARY 23, 2010

George called Sanford first thing in the morning and told him that he had a very bad cold and didn't want to come in "for fear of spreading it to the bride and the staff."

Sanford did not say, "Get well soon." He said, "I understand. It's for the best." And then he added, "Don't worry about any flowers for Lilyanne and the opera. She won't be needing any. You've done more for her in a few days than anyone has done for her - at least in this house - since I can remember."

George muttered, "Thanks. I may be sick tomorrow, too."

MONDAY, JANUARY 25, 2010

George did not notice, as he left his house to go to his office, that a blue Ford sedan was parked down the street.

He drove his pickup to the office, glad to note that this was the last day of the deLisle case.

Beryl had prepared the bill as far as she was able. "Sixteen more hours to go," she said. "And if you want me to close it out tomorrow, I'll handle it. Sensei told me yesterday that he wants to take a week off and go fishing in Key West. Marlin. Why don't you go with him? I'll hold down the fort here and at the temple."

"I don't know," George slowly answered. "I need to rest."

"Ok. You'll go to Key West and *not* do any marlin fishing. You can rest on the plane and on the beach. Maybe with a little luck it will rain and you won't even have to get out of bed."

The phone rang. Beryl answered. A male voice asked, "Is George there?" Beryl said that he was and handed George the receiver. But there was no one on the line when he answered. The caller had hung up. George shrugged and gave her the phone.

The blue sedan that had been parked down the street from his house, pulled into his driveway. A blonde man, wearing a neat business suit, got out of the car, walked up to George's front door, unlocked it, and let himself in.

The man hesitated, confused by the array of empty shelves and tables that filled the living and dining rooms. He went back to the kitchen and, finding George's corner bed, went to the prescription bottles that were on the sink. He opened each capsule in his night time joint prescription bottle, emptied the contents into the sink, and replaced the contents with oxycodone powder.

Beryl had left the office to tend to another case and George, glad to be back to his old routine, tended his sick plants in the window.

At eleven thirty the phone rang. George answered and was surprised to hear Cecelia Smith's tone of voice. She wanted a few words with him.

"What can I do for you?" he asked.

"I hardly know what to say, Mr. Wagner. I have been told on good authority that you have been working undercover in my hothouse, that your true purpose in accepting a position here was to spy on my family. I want to hear for myself that it is not true."

George was caught off-guard. How could she have found out about his investigative role? He kept Alicia Eckersley's position in mind. "It is partially true. That this office was running checks on your family, I cannot deny. But that I did intend to switch careers - if you can call it that - is true. Beryl, my partner, did most of the investigation. I worked in the hothouse and had no intention of leaving."

"Who hired your company to spy on us?"

"You know I cannot tell you that."

"I insist or else I shall get the information I want from Alicia Eckersley."

"Her connection to this is incidental. You needn't bother her. And if you use your imagination you can divine who it is who hired us and why."

"Do you mean the Contesse? She would stoop to this?"

"It's no different from anything you would do to protect your family. She didn't know Everett Smith from Adam Smith. And she didn't want to indulge in gossip. So she did the correct thing. She hired a private - the emphasis is on 'private' - firm to see if your family was suitable. Alicia Eckersley had only good things to say about you, but the countess wanted them verified."

"What precisely did you verify?"

George sighed. Reluctantly he answered. "Beryl verified that Lilyanne was in a convent for five years and not in a drug treatment program or lunatic asylum or state prison, and that she was a decent girl of great charm and intelligence with a pleasing personality and no sordid history whatsoever. Beryl also verified your credit rating which anyone could have done. I verified that you did have a prized orchid collection and that your family has occupied Tarleton for generations. In short, that you were not *nouveau riche*.

"Alicia Eckersley had mentioned to me that there was a job opening at Tarleton. My own collection is at her country estate. Her gardener is a good man with orchids so there wasn't much for me to do. She knew I wanted to devote my time to orchid hybridization, and when she heard that you were looking for someone, she called me. She certainly didn't know that this would end up with my being employed by the Contesse deLisle.

"Incidentally, the Countess got our official interim report. She was relieved to know that your family is above reproach. I understand why you're upset, and I apologize for the subterfuge."

"You can easily apologize for the subterfuge, but what can you say about the gossip you initiated?" She grew noticeably more angry. "You say 'private' but that is not how you conducted your affairs. Everyone is talking about the Smiths being under investigation. We've even heard that the government suspects we're growing illegal plants in the hothouse. You have subjected my family to ridicule and to suspicion of criminal activity. Mr. Wagner, your employment here is terminated."

George sighed. "Well," he said, "I don't have any of my own property at Tarleton. If your new man wants any information from me, he can call. Or, if you can't get anyone immediately, I'll be happy to come out and oversee things until you have a reliable replacement." He heard the phone click. His voice trailed off into space. "Just... call me..."

George immediately called Beryl on her cell to tell her about the call from Cecelia Smith. "Give Alicia Eckersley a call and bring her 'up to speed' about this latest development."

"How did they find out you were an investigator? Alicia will ask me."

"Beats me," said George quizzically. "I didn't give anybody any clue. I just don't know, and I didn't get the chance to ask her how she found out. The truth is that I had to get the hell out of there, and I don't give a damn who blew my cover."

He shuffled papers around and tried to focus his attention on something other than the deLisle case; but he did not succeed. Something was wrong. He began to talk to his plants. "I am missing something. What the hell is it that I can't see?" The plants had no answers.

He closed the office, drove home and parked in the driveway as usual. He sat in his truck and stared at the garage door. For eight years the garage had been filled with the furniture that he removed from his living room, dining room and den to make room for all the orchid plants that arrived when he returned from rehab.

While he was in the hospital, his wife divorced him, leaving him everything except their children. She had paid a plant nursery to care for her orchid collection until George was able to accept it. When that time came, the collection of 100 plants had grown to 367. He had to buy metal tables and shelves to accommodate them.

Though he had recently moved the plants to the Eckersley's hothouse, the empty tables and shelves, rusted and mismatched, were still in place. He ceased to notice them, or the stained rug and bare windows.

He no longer used the upstairs of his home. He used the kitchen as a bachelor's apartment. He kept a Tv, a recliner, small table and lamp, and his old kitchen set. He put a bed in the corner, near the sliding doors that opened onto the patio. That was it and until recently, that had been enough.

He got a Coke out of the refrigerator and found a movie on Tv. His shoulder began to ache. He nuked a Tv dinner, watched another movie, took his evening medications, and went to bed. Soon he sank into a deep and distant oblivion.

He did not know that Martin Shannon had dropped Eric off outside, and that Eric had entered his pickup truck, started the engine, and driven it away.

People turned to look at Lilyanne as she entered the lobby of the opera house. Felice and James Barton confided to each other that they never expected to be dull wallflowers while all the admiring looks were directed to Lilyanne Smith - of all people!

At the start of *Gotterdammerung's* second intermission at 10:45 p.m., Henri purchased two champagne cocktails (all that he could carry) for himself and Lilyanne. No one saw him deftly empty a small vial into her drink. James had also gone to the bar. Henri called Lilyanne aside. "Let's drink a toast to 'us,'" he said. "Down the hatch!" He emptied his glass and insisted that she do the same.

Downstairs in the lobby, a nicely dressed, white haired woman, approached the usher who stood at the base of the mezzanine staircase. She handed him a business card and a one hundred dollar bill, saying innocently, "A gentleman waiting outside in his car - he cannot park it - it's a kind of small truck - well, he asked me to give you this as payment for giving his card to the lady in Box 3. He said it is an urgent matter and that you shouldn't let anyone else know that you're giving her the card. She's wearing a green velvet gown and a lot of jewelry. Just escort her to the lobby entrance."

"Yes," he said, "I know exactly who she is. They've just come out for second intermission. She's probably out in the hall. I'll give it to her now. And thank you!" He climbed the stairs and immediately saw Lilyanne. Cautiously, he went to her and relayed the message. The card was George's business card. On the back it read, "Lilyanne, I must talk to you. It is urgent. Come outside and stand at the curb. Don't tell anyone. George."

Henri had engaged James and Felice in a spirited discussion about the Immolation Scene that they would soon be seeing. "I know it bar by bar," he said.

James asked, "Have you seen it at Bayreuth?"

Henri sighed, "My mother knows the Wagner family. We rarely miss an opening - and if we don't see it there, we see it in Sydney or Seattle, London or Los Angeles, Adelaide or- well, you get the picture."

James raised his eyebrows, "You really must like it."

Henri gave him a sly look. "For years I didn't like it, but then I learned to sleep with my eyes wide open and my ears closed tight - I don't see or hear anything. You'd be surprised… when you're comatose you don't mind it at all." Both men laughed.

James leaned forward and in a low voice said, "I'm sure you know Mark Twain's line, 'Wagner's music is not as bad as it sounds.'" Henri said that he did know the line and that he wasn't sure he agreed with it. They laughed and Henri countered with a line of Rossini's which he whispered to James. Again they laughed so heartily that Felice insisted that they tell her what was so funny.

Lilyanne became nervous. She didn't know how to respond to the usher; but when she looked around for Henri to ask what she should do, he was huddled with James and Felice and they were laughing together. She also felt a little warm and thought that going out into the cold air to see George was a good idea. "I'll go down right now," she said to the usher who immediately led her down the stairs, through the lobby, and to the top of the exterior stairs that led down to the sidewalk.

The passenger door to a pickup truck opened and Lilyanne hurried to it. The driver who wore a hooded sweat jersey extended a gloved hand to her and she awkwardly climbed into the truck. "George?" she asked as the driver reached across her to shut the door. Suddenly, an ether-saturated mask was pressed over her nose and mouth by an unseen hand. Someone held her arms. She struggled for a minute. Then she ceased being frantic and slumped into unconsciousness.

The truck drove away from the opera house. Three blocks away it pulled into the opened gateway of the fenced back yard of a corner house on Spruce Street. A cream colored limousine was parked inside. The gate closed behind the truck.

Charlotte got out of the back seat and took off her old lady's white wig and steel rimmed glasses. Everything had already been prepared for the operation. Inside the house, lying neatly on the floor in four separate piles were the wigs, jewelry, and items of disguise that the two men would use as Charlotte photographed them with two digital cameras. On the kitchen table were jeweler's tools, equipment, a high-intensity light, and a suitcase filled with green glass and zircon stones in various sizes and cuts.

Charlotte stripped off Lilyanne's jewelry and put the pieces on the table as Martin put on a jeweler's eyepiece and immediately set to work removing the stones and replacing them with glass substitutes.

Eric removed Lilyanne's clothing. Her limp body offered no resistance.

While Charlotte adjusted the lights, Eric put on a dark brown shoulder length wig; an upper dental plate; adhesive side burns; darkened his eyebrows; and put on a gaudy wristwatch and a gold necklace. Standing naked in the living room, he pulled the combs and pins from Lilyanne's hair and re-arranged the styling.

Charlotte dabbed instant glue onto the girl's finger pads and eyelids, and ordered, "Fellatio first." Then she put Lilyanne on her knees, and to hold her body upright, Eric's right hand clasped the girl's hair on the side away from the camera's view. Charlotte pressed the girl's fingers on Eric's buttocks until they adhered and then lifted her eyelids, carefully gluing them so that Lilyanne's eyes appeared to be naturally open.

As Charlotte found the angle from which she would photograph the scene, Eric filled the girl's mouth with his penis. If the photos came out as planned, the girl would be looking up admiringly at this man with the long brown hair. Charlotte took half a dozen photos from different angles, all of which showed the girl's unmistakable scars. She changed cameras and took more photographs. The girl's fingers were pulled away from his skin, leaving red areas of glue residue that had to be removed with acetone and cosmetically powdered. Charlotte put lubricating drops into Lilyanne's eyes.

As he prepared for his positional change, Charlotte called for Martin to take his turn. He left his work of removing real stones in Lilyanne's jewelry and replacing them with fakes. Martin put on a dreadlocks style wig, a fake mustache, an African bead necklace, and a stainless steel diver's watch. "Fellatio," Charlotte said calmly, and the process was repeated.

Eric put on a condom. He and Charlotte placed Lilyanne into an upholstered chair, splaying her legs over the arm rests. She cleverly taped the sides of Lilyanne's cheeks, pulling the skin back just enough to make it appear that the girl was in ecstasy, and then she covered the tape with curls. She again dabbed the girl's finger pads with glue and pressed them onto his shoulders. "Now, intercourse!" He thrust himself hard into her. "I got her cherry," he said. Charlotte laughed. "Congratulations."

As Eric changed his disguise, Martin repeated the actions. The reflective lights were focussed on a couch on the other side of the room.

Eric now wore a curly dark blonde wig that was tied, colonial style, at the back of his neck. He removed his upper dental plate, put in a lower one, inserted cheek pads, put a spring type ring earring in his right ear, and a different watch on his right wrist, giving himself an entirely different appearance. He put wet theatrical-quality decalcomania tattoos onto his right upper arm as Charlotte used a hair dryer to "fix" the color of the tattoo paper.

Eric then laid the girl upon the couch, putting her hands behind her head. Using both cameras, Charlotte photographed Lilyanne and Eric in a variety of obscene poses. When she was finished, she put more eye drops in the girl's eyes. "You're done," she said. Eric cleaned off the decalcomania and worked in the kitchen, removing and replacing stones.

She put a bedspread over the couch, carefully concealing all the parts of the couch. She grabbed Lilyanne's hair and with a brush swept the curls out into a wild arrangement and then covered her lips with a dark lipstick. Lilyanne began to moan and to flail her arms.

"Bring that ether mask. Drop more onto the gauze," Charlotte called.

The ether bottle and mask had been put in the bathroom. Martin quickly brought them to the stirring girl and clamped the mask over her nose. She struggled and as he held the mask and opened the bottle of ether, he spilled some of it on her hair. "Tell Eric to open the kitchen window," he said, "or I'll be on the floor out cold."

Pushing and pulling Lilyanne's limp body into various poses with the help of instant glue, he proceeded to pose for the photographs that Charlotte directed.

Then he exchanged his wig for a more African "fro" style and put a big loop earring in his right ear, inserted an upper dental plate, and changed his jewelry to a gold watch, bracelet, and a gold chain necklace.

Charlotte put Lilyanne face-down on the floor, propping her buttocks up with a pillow She put a studded dog collar on her neck and handcuffs on her wrists, securing them to the legs of the couch. With an erasable red felt pen drew stripes on her buttocks and turned her face to the camera as she posed Martin with a cat-o-nine tails whip. She took a dozen different shots and then announced, "We've got enough!" Martin resumed his work of switching the stones.

Charlotte cleaned the red stripes off Lilyanne's buttocks, released the handcuffs, unbuckled the dog collar, reassembled her hair as nearly as possible to its original style, and dressed her.

Henri had taken his seat in the opera box, waiting for Felice to return from seeking Lilyanne in one of the lady's rooms. "Perhaps she felt ill from the excitement and needed air but didn't want to distress me." He feigned increasing concern as the minutes passed. Felice returned with no news. She had searched each lady's room and Lilyanne was not in any of them. Finally, during Siegfried's funeral march, he got up, left the box, and questioned several ushers. He returned to the box just before the Immolation Scene and called Eric.

Eric was rubbing his arm with a bleaching cloth as his phone rang. He continued to rub as he said, "Yes, sir." Henri sounded frantic. "Miss Smith is missing! She was seen getting into one of those pickup trucks, a dark colored one. Drive around and look to see that they're not parked somewhere talking. Maybe she fell ill. Who knows what could have happened to her? Where are you now? Well, start from there, you're only a couple of blocks away. Circle around and keep in touch. The opera will soon be over and people will be leaving. We'll look around this block. Do not call the police or tell anybody what you're doing. This must be kept quiet! Get a list of the area hospitals. Call their Emergency Rooms and ask if a lady has been brought in." He gasped, "Oh, my God, my God! What could have happened to her?"

"Don't worry, Sir," he said. "We'll find her." He was close enough to Henri to be in the same microwave tower area. "Yes, sir," he said, "I'm turning onto Spruce Street now."

Eric finished removing the decal on his arm, dressed in his chauffeur's uniform, and went into the kitchen to help with the jewelry replacements. Martin put on his street clothes with the hooded jacket.

Nearly two hours passed since Lilyanne had been picked up outside the opera house.

Charlotte quickly dressed in clothing appropriate to her aristocratic station. "How are the pieces?" she called.

Martin answered. "We've got all the major stones switched."

Charlotte called, in an imitation of the final words of *Gotterdammerung*, Hagen's "'Zuruck vom Ring!' I want that emerald engagement ring!"

Martin picked it up and held it above his head as Charlotte grabbed it and put it in her purse. She gathered all the stolen stones and put them in an envelope which she also dropped into her purse. She and Eric finished dressing Lilyanne then put her bracelet, earrings, tiara, and necklace on. "Martin, my dear, please take the lady up to her friend's house. I'll follow in the Ford." She picked up the case that contained the collection of fake stones and jeweler's tools, placed the cameras she had used inside it, and took the case with her as she got into the Ford sedan parked outside at the curb.

Martin picked up Lilyanne and carried her out the back door. He placed her in the pickup's passenger seat and secured her seat belt. As he pulled out into the street and headed for the Schuylkill Expressway, Charlotte followed close behind.

Eric locked the house and after making certain that they had left nothing inside, he exited the premises, returned to lock the fence gate, and drove the limousine into the street. Then he called Henri. "Finally, he said, "I've gotten through to you, sir. I kept get--."

Henri cut him off. "It's my fault. I've been calling everywhere."

Eric assured him that he was now on Locust street again and there was no sign of a pickup truck. "I went up to one truck that had a couple of lovers in it and I was nearly shot when I startled them."

Henri had been driving in James and Felice's car. "It's time for me to go back to Tarleton. Lilyanne is still not home. Her parents are distraught. Come and pick me up. I'm at.." he looked out the window at the street signs, "Chestnut and Broad Street."

Eric said, "Very good, sir. I will be there shortly."

TUESDAY, JANUARY 26, 2010

It was strange to see so many lights on at Tarleton House in the middle of the night on a weekday night. No one had thought to alert the gatekeeper and the old man had to be awakened when the limousine pulled into the drive at 3:30 a.m. Finally the gate swung open and the limousine followed by James and Felice's BMW continued the drive to the portico. Cecelia and Everett Smith came out onto the portico to meet them.

Henri got out of the limousine and called, "Have you heard anything?"

"No," said Everett. "What has happened? I want the entire story - start to finish."

They all went inside. Henri, his eyes red and swollen from hand lotion he had purposely rubbed into them, reviewed the incident, as tears ran down his cheeks. "Lilyanne had been happily drinking a champagne cocktail and we were all laughing when an usher gave her a business card." He shuddered and blew his nose. "The usher hadn't read the card and could tell us only that an elderly lady had passed it on with a request to give it to the lady in green velvet. Another usher saw her leave the opera house and go down onto the sidewalk and then to get into a dark, four door pickup truck. The truck was apparently waiting for her since the front passenger door was pushed open as she approached the truck." He whined and wiped his eyes. "No one knew anything more. Both my limousine and the Barton's BMW circled the area for more than an hour. We called hospitals!" he sniffed. "Lilyanne had not been brought into any of them."

Cecelia insisted, "She doesn't know anyone. Why would she have gone out?"

Henri was close to fainting from the strain. "Someone lured her out! But who? It's all my fault. I forced the alcohol on her. Should we call the police?"

"No!" Cecelia was quick to veto that suggestion. "An official inquiry means scandal! And didn't the man I fired... the hothouse keeper... drive a truck?"

Sanford was standing at the side of the room, saying nothing. At the mention of the truck, he interjected, "Yes. Mr. Wagner did drive a pickup truck. He used to be with the Philadelphia Police. Perhaps he can be of help."

"Well, go get his number!" she demanded. Sanford reached into an inside jacket pocket and retrieved a small notebook. "Here it is. Shall I ring him for you now?"

"Of course, you fool! Why else would I have wanted the number?"

"Can you not be civil?" Everett shouted. "Why, at every crisis, must your tongue thrash about like a drowning child!"

Cecelia hissed, "We will discuss this matter later!"

"Excuse me, Madam, but Mr. Wagner's phone has gone to voice mail. Should I leave a message?"

"No. We'll call again," Everett said. "Thank you, Sanford. You can retire now if you wish."

As Sanford bowed and turned to leave the room, James Barton tried to calm everyone by offering a temporary solution. "She's with someone she knew. Why don't we all go home and wait for morning. If she still is not home, we can call every hospital again and then we can make discreet police inquiries. We can probably locate the hothouse keeper although saying that she got into a dark colored pickup truck hardly implicates him."

Henri paced back and forth. "Thank God my mother keeps her cellphone shut off. She won't turn it on until she calls down for breakfast." He flopped down in a stuffed chair. "I'm exhausted and I don't know what to do. I agree. I don't want scandal if it's nothing serious. It will plague my darling girl for years. You know how people talk - and she is so sensitive."

He covered his face with his hands. "Oh, Holy Mother, pray for us. Oh, Lord Jesus, keep her safe."

James and Felice Barton went to the door. "Let's all pray tonight," James said as they entered the foyer and quickly headed for the front door.

"If only the usher had read the card!" Henri moaned. "Of all times for an employee to be discreet!"

"All right," said Everett. "Let us hope for the best and pray. We can all meet here in the morning at, say, 9 a.m.? We'll keep all our phones on. If anyone hears anything, please contact me."

Everyone agreed.

Lilyanne regained consciousness gradually. The truck grew cold and she began to shiver - which helped her to awaken. She did not know where she was or how she had gotten there.

She unbuckled her seat belt and tried the door. It opened and she looked around, recognizing nothing. Everything seemed blurred. She squinted at the house number and finally saw that it was number 1345, but that meant nothing to her. There was a name printed on a gnome figurine on the lawn. She went to it and read the name, "Wagner." She turned and stumbled towards the front door. She pushed the door bell and heard it ring. Again she pushed the bell. Finally she walked to the patio at the side of the house and tried to look through the glass sliding doors. A nightlight in the room illuminated a figure in a bed. She began to pound on the glass door. George sat up in bed and looked around dumbly. He saw Lilyanne at the door, but he was too groggy to make sense of what he was seeing. Finally he got up and went to the glass and with squinting eyes looked at her. He quickly composed himself and slid open the door. Lilyanne fell into his arms shivering and crying. She was seriously cold, he realized. He put her in his bed and wrapped her in his blanket which was still warm.

He sat beside her until she felt warm and could speak coherently. Then he picked her up and carried her to the kitchen table, sat her in a chair, and put a kettle on for tea. He also put several pastries into the microwave.

It was dawn. He could see how blotched her face was, the redness of her eyelids and her fingers and hands. "I think we should call your mother and father. They're probably frantic. And Henri, too."

"No... wait," she said. "What did you want when you came to the opera?"

"I didn't come to the opera. What are you talking about?"

"You sent me your card. I put it in my purse. Where is my purse? Maybe I left it in your truck."

"What would it be doing in *my* truck?" He put on jeans, shirt, socks and shoes, picked up his keys, and went outside to check the truck. He found her purse on the floor. Still wondering how and when she got to his house, he put his hand on the bonnet and felt the engine's warmth. Then he checked the odometer and the fuel level. The truck had less than a quarter tank. It should have had more.

He brought the purse into the kitchen. "You look awful," he said to her. "What the hell is going on?"

"You asked me to come out to your truck."

"Lilyanne... I've been here all night! I don't know what you're talking about. Who drove you here in my truck?"

She opened her purse and found the card. She gave it to George. "Here.. look.."

"This is my card, but I did not write this message. And how the hell did you get into my truck?"

"I don't know. I don't know."

"What's the last thing you remember?"

"Getting into your truck outside the opera house."

"We've got to call your parents" He picked up his phone and called the Smiths. Everett Smith answered. "Who is this?"

George was a little surprised by his aggressive attitude. "I'm calling to let you know that your daughter is here at my house. She woke up in my pickup outside in the driveway and doesn't know how she got here."

Everett asked to speak to her. Confused, George listened to her side of the conversation and tried to understand. "Daddy?" "I don't know." Her head wobbled. "I don't know. I don't feel good, Daddy." She could hear her mother hysterically shout that she should call Henri. She retched. "No. I don't know what to say." She handed the phone to George. "My father wants you to take me home." She gagged. "I'm sick," she gasped. "Where's the bathroom?"

George took the phone. "I'll get her home as soon as possible. She's sick. I'll call you back as soon as I can. Meanwhile she's ok. Don't worry." He hung up the phone and guided Lilyanne to the bathroom.

He called Beryl. "I'll be right there. My son's home. I'll leave him a note." She did not like the sound of his voice. "I think you should call Percy, too."

George did not argue. He hit the speed dial for Sensei. The priest answered and agreed to come immediately. When George ended the call he began to notice that he, too, didn't feel well.

A half hour later, Sensei arrived, wearing religious garb. Beryl pulled up behind him.

Sensei unlocked the front door and they entered the house, going directly to the kitchen.

Sensei looked at George and Lilyanne. "My God, man. You two look like you've been hit by a bus. But you're not black and blue."

"Bless me, Father," George said wearily, "even though I haven't sinned."

"I hope you can prove that," Sensei joked, looking at Lilyanne. "What happened?"

Beryl went immediately to the girl. "We've never met. I'm George's partner, Beryl Tilson. What happened to you last night? Your face and your hands… you're all blotchy. Red. Your eye lids look like they've been burned." She lifted the girl's hands and smelled them. "They have a chemical smell. And you don't remember?"

Lilyanne looked at her hands. "They feel burned. They hurt. My eyes feel funny, too. And my eyelids hurt. And I feel sick to my stomach. I need to go back to the bathroom again."

"I'll help you," Beryl said. As she put her arm around the smaller girl to support her, her nose got close to the girl's head. "Do I detect ether?

Did someone use ether on you?" She called to the priest. "Sensei, come here and smell her hair."

The priest jumped up from his chair and put his face in the girl's hair. "It's ether, all right. There's not another smell like it."

Lilyanne gagged urgently. Beryl quickly pushed her into the bathroom to let her vomit the tea George had given her, plus a copious amount of bile.

When they returned to the kitchen Beryl asked, "Do you want to stay here a little longer or do you want me to take you home now."

Lilyanne began to cry. "I want to stay here."

Beryl got her phone and called Tarleton House. When Everett answered she said in a business-like manner, "I'm Beryl Tilson, George Wagner's partner. Lilyanne is sick. She has the smell of ether in her hair. She just vomited. Personally, I think I should take her to the hospital."

"Ether? My God! What are you saying? Did someone operate on her?"

"No, Mr. Smith, she's still got both of her kidneys, if that's what you're thinking. To me it looks like she's been drugged. I'll take her to the hospital and keep you apprised of her condition."

"Please watch over her," he said, as Cecelia was shouting that he should find out where specifically she'd be taken. Everett ignored his wife. "Thank you for taking care of her. Call me," he said quickly and hung up.

"Let's take her to the hospital," Beryl said. "Something bad happened to this girl."

"Look at George," Sensei said. "Something's wrong with him, too. He's groggy. Let's take them both."

Beryl agreed. "We can take my car. The nearest hospital is First Baptist."

At the Emergency Room, an intern examined Lilyanne and thought she should be admitted. Beryl asked him if he could smell ether and he said that he could. He wanted to run a variety of blood tests. Her heart was beating irregularly and her blood pressure was extremely low. As the doctor examined George he noted a slightly lower blood pressure. He also asked the technician to draw blood from George. "Something is wrong with this man, too," he said, shining a light into George's eyes. "His pupils aren't reacting properly. He's been drugged."

"Impossible," George said. "I'm a recovering addict. I don't go near the stuff." He opened his shirt and showed the intern the extensive scarring of his shoulder and back. "And this, too," he said, pulling up his pant leg to show the scarring on his knee. "Gun shot. I'm a former police investigator." He presented his medical insurance cards to the clerk.

The doctor was satisfied. "I think you should call your own physician as soon as you can. But I don't think you require admission right now. Still, we'll do some blood studies. I've got to report this, but it's just a formality in your case. And by the way, I can see why the pain killers got to you. Jesus." He took both of George's hands and held them up. "Look at this," he said to a nurse. "This is what damage to the brachial plexus can do."

Sensei gave the admissions clerk his credit card and said that the girl was his daughter, Lily Wong. Beryl told her to use that name if anyone spoke to her. While the paperwork was being processed, Lilyanne's garments were exchanged for a hospital gown, and her evening gown, shoes, bag, and jewelry were put into a bag and given to Beryl. The nurse called Beryl aside, "There's blood in her panties and her vaginal area is bruised. We should do a rape kit." Lilyanne made the Sign of the Cross and scribbled a name for permission to have the rape test.

The examining physician determined that there was no semen present and that it appeared to be a rupture of the hymen and, he added, extremely rough sex.

"Don't tell my family," Lilyanne whispered. She began to cry, and the doctor gave her a sedative. Beryl stayed with her until she fell asleep.

George had fallen asleep as he and Sensei waited for Beryl to return. When she did return, Sensei said, "Let's get this guy home to bed, and, if somebody got his car keys, his house and office keys were on the same ring. Shouldn't you get your locks rekeyed?"

"Not only his house and office, but the keys to my apartment were on the ring, too. I'll call a locksmith and get the locks re-keyed immediately. What about the temple?"

"That, too. Send the locksmith to my place when he's finished. Let's get him home and then we'll see where we think we might be vulnerable."

George had awakened enough to comment. "The temple keys are in the cookie jar. Let's get me over to the desk so I can sign myself out."

Beryl scrolled through her iPhone's list of locksmiths. "I'll also let Jack know what's happening."

At George's house, Beryl again called Tarleton House. Cecelia Smith immediately demanded, "Who is this?"

"I'm the person who's helping Lilyanne. I called before. If you don't calm down and compose yourself, I will hang up."

Cecilia grunted. "Very well," she said. "Where is my daughter?"

"She is in the hospital. She was admitted because she was indicating a serious reaction to drugs. The doctor thought that if all went well, she could be released tomorrow, although the results of the toxicology tests might take a few weeks. She does not want to come home to Tarleton immediately. At least that is what she told me today. She may feel differently tomorrow."

"What hospital is she in?"

"I'm sorry but I can't tell you that. I can ask her to call you, if you like. But she's over twenty-one years old and can make her own decisions. I am asking you not to make things worse."

"So you, a stranger, prefer to make her decisions, rather than her parents."

"She was not unconscious. She signed all her forms. I did what her attending physician recommended. No more, no less. If she is released tomorrow she will need regular clothing. They took her gown, shoes, and jewelry off and gave them to me. If you will be kind enough to put together a suitable set of shoes and garments, I will come there now and we can exchange the clothing."

Beryl waited for her response, but Cecelia said nothing. "Look," Beryl said finally, "someone else needs my attention. I need to make calls. So make up your mind."

"Very well," Cecelia conceded, "I'll get some clothing ready." Beryl said simply, "Thank you. I'll be there at noon." Beryl immediately called George's doctor and left a message with his receptionist.

She looked worried. "Sensei, I don't want to go out there alone. I'll ask Jack if he can come up here and sit with George. Would you come with me?"

"Sure," he said. Beryl called her son who, having no car, had to be picked up by her and brought back to George's house.

Beryl and Sensei were immediately passed through the gate. They parked along side the other cars in front of the portico. As they mounted the steps, Sensei whispered, "For the girl's sake, try to keep cool."

Sanford opened the door for them even before they knocked. They followed him into the drawing room and looked at the strange group of faces that confronted them. Henri, the Contesse, James and Felice Barton, Cecelia and Everett Smith stared at them, not knowing what to say.

The only face Beryl recognized was the Countess. She nodded with a faint smile, but the woman ignored the greeting and disdainfully turned away.

In measured syllables Cecelia Smith asked, "Do you mind telling me what has happened to my daughter? And who is this person in an oriental costume?"

Beryl knew that protocol requires that the person of lower rank is presented to the person of higher rank. She therefore said, "I take it that you're Cecelia Smith. So nice to finally meet you." She turned to Percy, "Sensei, may I present Lilyanne's mother, Mrs. Everett Smith. Mrs. Smith, this is the Reverend Shi Yao Feng who very kindly paid for your daughter's medical care."

Everett Smith growled through gritted teeth, *"Will somebody tell me what has happened to my daughter!"*

"For God's sake," Henri begged Beryl, "are you enjoying playing this sick 'cat and mouse' game of yours. Where is my Lilyanne? What have you done with her?"

"She is fine. She is in a hospital. More than likely, she'll be released tomorrow."

Henri stood up. "I insist that you take me to her immediately."

Beryl tried to sound reasonable. "I'm sorry, but I cannot do that. Her doctor wants her to sleep and since she also has been nauseous, I think she prefers to spend the day alone. I'll bring her here as soon as she thinks she's ready."

Henri held his head and walked to the fireplace. He seemed to be talking more to himself than anyone else. "Was she attacked? Beaten? Oh, it is all my fault. It is all my fault. I am to blame. I was negligent. How will she ever forgive me? I'm such a fool!"

Beryl looked around at the faces. The countess looked angry. Beryl tried to avert any unpleasantness. She held up the bag of clothing, and said to Cecelia, "I've got Lilyanne's evening wear here. Do you have her casual clothing ready?"

"In her bedroom," Cecelia said weakly. "Come upstairs with me and you can tell me which garments you think she would prefer."

Beryl followed her upstairs.

The two women sat on Lilyanne's bed. "There really isn't much to tell you except that somehow, someone sent her one of George's business cards which had a note written on the back, asking your daughter to come outside of the opera house during intermission--"

"Yes, yes, I know that. You say it was George? George Wagner's card?"

Beryl pulled out the staples and turned the bag upside down. She shook it, letting the contents fall upon the bed. "Here's her tiara, necklace, earrings, bracelet, gown, slip, shoes, stockings and purse." She opened the purse and looked inside. "Here's George's business card. The note is on the back. But I assure you, George did not send the note."

Cecelia was indignant. "And just how do you know he didn't lure her out of the opera house with this note? Was this some kind of repayment for my firing him?"

Beryl did not appreciate the tone or the accusation. "First, ever since he was shot in the right shoulder, he can barely write legibly. He cannot make neat little letters. If you don't believe me, have it analyzed by a forensic document examiner and talk to George's numerous physicians and physical therapists. Go ahead. Have it analyzed."

"He could have had someone write it for him."

"But he didn't, and you are heading for a law suit, my dear, and a lot of bad publicity. Be careful about the accusations you throw about in public. Something terrible has happened to your daughter. George is fond of her and in deference to him, I'm helping."

"The most terrible thing that has happened to her, as far as I can tell, is that you are trying to manage this situation to suit your associate's interests and not my daughter's. There are people downstairs who are demanding to see her for themselves. They need to be reassured."

Beryl sighed. "Is there no way I can reason with you? Is there no way that I can appeal to you - as one mother to another - to try to see this incident from Lilyanne's point of view. She is not used to such excitement. A confrontation with people who don't understand the situation will only worsen her emotional state. Just let her rest another day."

Cecelia was adamant. "A day's rest is not going to undo the damage she has already caused to this engagement!"

It was obvious to Beryl that no simple explanation was going to suffice. Without somebody in that house - somebody in authority - who knew the truth and would be the girl's ally, Lilyanne would never be able to withstand the kind of interrogation that these frenetic people would subject her to. "Mrs. Smith," Beryl said gently, "I'm going to tell you something that I promised I would keep to myself. But if there is one person in this whole drama who is truly needed at this moment, that person is you. You are her mother, and above all, she needs you."

Cecelia took a deep breath and prepared herself for even more bad news. "I'm listening," she said.

"You'll notice that her panties are missing from the pile of garments they removed at the hospital. There was blood in them. She had agreed to be given a rape test. They have her bloody panties in the hospital. I don't know if they will be used as evidence or not. She didn't want you and her father to know."

Cecelia Smith gasped. "Dear Lord! How could this have happened? Virginity was prerequisite!" She looked through the objects on the bed. She looked inside the purse. "Where is her engagement ring?"

"I never saw it. She was not wearing any rings. Another thing... her eyelids, hands, and fingers appear to have been burned somehow with some strange smelling chemical. And she had the noticeable odor of ether in her hair. This was confirmed by the doctor on duty at the hospital. They will be running HIV and other tests for sexually transmitted diseases."

Cecelia began to tremble. "Don't tell them downstairs. I beg you. Don't tell them downstairs."

"I won't. Just pull yourself together and give me the clothing. If she wants to come to my place tomorrow, I'll take her there or I'll bring her here. I'll give you my private number." She wrote her personal number on her card and handed it to the bewildered woman. "Let Lilyanne select for herself the people with whom she wants to discuss this ugly episode."

"Then I would like to speak to her before she enters this house and blurts out all the lascivious details. Four months out of the convent and already she's at the heart of a disaster!"

Cecelia went to the closet and returned with clothing that she placed in an overnight bag. Suddenly her teeth clenched and she seemed stronger. "Just ask for me when you call. I am the Tarleton of Tarleton House. Don't bother discussing this with my husband."

"I also won't bother blaming the victim," Beryl said pointedly.

"My dear, I know that she did not attack herself," Cecelia replied sarcastically. "She simply has a talent for catastrophe. Why did she allow herself to be lured out of the theater? It wasn't naiveté. It was simply bad manners. No wellborn woman would leave the side of her escort." Stoically, as if she were used to the frustration, she sighed, "And everything was going so well. No one is to know of this hospital business. It's bad enough that we'll have to conceal the hospital records."

"The priest is paying for her care and she was admitted as his daughter. Her name is not in the records. He'll go with me to get her out tomorrow, or whenever they think it's safe for her to go. I'll tell her that we talked. But please don't start nagging her for information. She doesn't know because she was drugged. Let her go back to being her sweet self. Maybe the lost ring will be accepted as the motive."

Cecelia said, "It would be easier to have taken her tiara than her ring." She glanced at the tiara then abruptly focussed on a particular stone. One of the prongs was not properly aligned. "Oh, God! Some of these large emeralds are loose, and they look more like glass!"

"Well, there's the motive for luring her out. Do you want to keep this quiet, too?"

"No," said Cecelia as her thoughts raced. "This gives her the perfect escape from scandal. She was robbed not raped! I'll act as if they were amateurs and did not really get the best stones. Meanwhile, I'll have the stones replaced. I'll tell Lilyanne the truth and that this was obviously the reason she was drugged. I'll say that she was innocently lured out of the opera house on a pretext that her father was outside with an urgent message. Then the thieves subdued her with chloroform. The reason she's in the hospital is that she's recovering from the mugging. The jewelry is insured and only the loss of her engagement ring really matters. She'll tell Henri that she feels horrible about his gorgeous ring but that our insurance should replace it." She sighed and congratulated herself for having "spun straw into gold."

As Beryl and Cecelia descended the stairs they could hear the arguments raging in the living room.

The countess was both annoyed and suspicious. "I fail to see how two champagne cocktails in the course of a five hour opera could possibly have intoxicated anyone. She made a conscious decision to leave your side."

Henri quickly reacted. "No, *Mamán*! I won't have Lilyanne blamed for anything! She is an innocent in all of this!"

"She was out all night with a man, for heaven's sake!"

"No she was not. She was taken to a hospital."

"And I suppose that solves everything," she snarled.

"It was I who put the champagne in her hand. James and Felice bear witness to that."

Felice spoke in a calming voice. "We mustn't lose sight of the fact that she is completely unused to alcohol as well as the excitement of so many admiring looks. We were all laughing about something silly when she left. We should have paid more attention to her."

"If she threw up, the fellow might have driven her someplace where she could recover."

Charlotte's voice oozed with contempt. "How nice. What a clever way to package something sordid. What is being concealed here? Two glasses of champagne? Or was she taking some sort of medication, a medication that interacted with alcohol? I insist upon knowing why a healthy young woman would become sickened by two glasses of champagne!"

Henri began to shout. "She is not a child and I am not a child. All this parental criticism is uncalled for. She shall be *my* wife. We are engaged now and if she will still have me, *she shall be my wife!* That is final, *Maman!* Please don't let this little incident disturb our relationshp. I love you *Mamán!* But a man cannot put his mother before his wife. Let's end these foolish suspicions. *Mamán!* Please! I love her!"

Cecelia stood in the doorway. "It may interest all of you to know that the mystery has been solved. My daughter was lured out of the Opera because she was told that her father was out at the curb with an urgent message for her. The usher told her that he was double-parked and could not wait. She had to come immediately. And then when she went to the vehicle that the usher innocently indicated that her father was in, she was chloroformed and mugged of some of her emerald and diamond jewelry. She is in the hospital now, just as a precaution. She'll be released today. There is no cause for alarm. She is well and the jewelry is insured. You can all cease debating about my daughter's conduct."

As Beryl passed James Barton she stopped to say, "I need to talk to you privately."

"Please, take my card," he said. He wrote his private number on it.

As they drove back to the office, Jack called. "We've got a small problem. George's doctor called and wants me to bring him to his office right away. Can I drive him there in George's truck?"

"No! Don't touch George's truck. It needs to be fingerprinted. Don't let anyone near the truck."

Sensei took the phone. "Take my car. George has keys to it. They're in the cookie jar on the kitchen counter."

Sensei Percy Wong and Beryl sat in George's kitchen and tried to connect the events of the last twenty-four hours. Nothing came together in any sensible way.

Sensei was puzzled about George's condition. "I know we'll learn more when Jack brings him back, but meanwhile, I think we ought to take a look at George's prescriptions. I've seen him in pain and I've seen him sleepy. But he's groggy. He felt groggy the other day, too."

Beryl agreed. She brought the bottles from the bathroom. They looked at the capsules but had nothing to compare them to. "He might have taken extra pills," Sensei said.

While they looked at the capsules, George and Jack returned from the doctor's office.

George was feeling better. "The doc wants me to take the two prescription bottles down to the forensic lab. He wrote up an order to have them analyzed. Meanwhile I had to get new prescriptions filled." He put the drug store bag on the table.

Sensei reached for it and took the two prescription bottles and opened them to compare their contents to the ones taken from the bathroom. One prescription contained identical powder. But the other contained completely different powder. "Uh, oh," he said. "Here's the problem."

George rubbed his face. "I've got to get back to bed."

The group dispersed. Sensei returned to the Zen Temple. Beryl took Jack home so that he could pick up his bags and she could then drive him to the airport. Then she went to the hospital to see Lilyanne.

Lilyanne's face and hands were covered with a medicinal cream. "How did Henri take the news that I'm here?" she asked Beryl.

"You'll have to ask your mother for details. Some of the emeralds in your jewelry were replaced with glass. Robbery seems to have been the reason for your abduction. Your mother told everyone that it was your father who had an urgent message for you. I told Henri you were safe and were just being held overnight. He was very relieved. His mother still had a fit about you leaving the opera, but I think that Henri made a point of saying that it was probably *Gotterdammerung* for five hours that all on its own influenced you to get some air."

Lilyanne grinned. "It was pretty boring."

"Did they determine what kind of chemical burn you had?"

"No. They are treating it with a neutral compound. It's been helping."

"You probably will be released tomorrow. I had a private talk with your mother. I felt it necessary to confide the extent of the assault. I had no alternative. Everyone was in such a frenzy, insisting on seeing you and interrogating you, and I felt it was the only way to call off the dogs. Your mom seemed to understand. She begged me not to tell Henri about the rape kit. I begged *her* not to tell *anyone*."

"I'm glad she knows. It's better if we can be truthful about it."

"Yes, and now that she knows the whole story, she can let the focus fall on the robbery motive."

"What did Henri say about my ring?"

"He didn't care about it at all."

"What about the hospital bill?"

"Sensei paid the bill in full. He had you admitted as his daughter, Lily Wong. If there are any further charges, he'll pay. I'm sure that your family will repay him."

"You know, this morning I forgot my secret name. I wondered why the nurse kept calling me Mizzwong. 'Good morning misswong.' Then

I remembered I was Mizzwong. And of course, we'll be sure to repay Sensei."

"It's up to you to decide where you want to go. You can come home with me or go home to Tarleton. You should talk to Henri. He'll understand whatever you choose."

"I don't know what to do. Maybe I should talk to George."

"George isn't at Tarleton anymore. He was fired. But you can reach him at home or the office."

"Fired?"

"The truth is that the Contesse engaged us to verify that your family was legitimate - rich and high class enough for Henri. George gave her a good report, but somehow your mother learned that he was investigating the family and got very angry."

"Then I'll stay with you for a couple of days, but I'd still like to talk to George."

"If the doctor lets you go tomorrow, you can spend the night at my apartment, which is just over the office. We'll all rest and relax for a day and night, and then in the morning, I'll take you back to Tarleton. I think your mother will be happy to see you without the red blotches."

Beryl left the overnight bag beside Lilyanne's bed and returned to her apartment.

WEDNESDAY, JANUARY 27, 2010

George got to the office early and turned his attention to his plants in the window. He was whistling as he gently aerated the orchid roots. He had decided to start a new life. And in this life there would be nothing but flowers. He would devote more time to the serious study of hybridization. There were college extension courses he could take. He might have time to register for the next course. Botany. He'd be a botanist. He could talk "pistils and stamens" with the best of them - but he lacked academic credentials. Hell, he could take regular courses on the internet. He needed to know more about dominant and recessive genes. And plant diseases, too. He was only forty-three. He'd take his religion more seriously. He'd take monastic vows: the life pared down to basics. Yes, a lay ordained monk. Zen's answer to the *Bird Man of Alcatraz.*

In the kitchen at the rear of the office, he heard footsteps overhead as he mixed orchid food with bottled water. That would be Beryl upstairs, making her morning tea. He heard a chair scrape the floor. She'd be sitting down now to drink it. It was comforting to have her living so close by. And then he heard another chair scrape the floor and the unmistakable sound of two women laughing. He looked up at the ceiling until he nearly lost his balance. Then he grabbed the edge of the sink and leaned on it; and slowly, silently, his happy expression contorted into anguish.

He was still bent over the sink when Beryl opened her apartment door and called down to him, "George! Lily's here. Do you want us to bring tea down?"

Before he could answer, he forced himself to relax and exhale. Then he called, "No, you go ahead. I'm tending the patients."

"Say! Did you drive your pickup here?" Beryl called. It was more of an accusation than a question.

"No. Perce came up and got me early, before he opened the Temple. Some guys from forensics are going over my truck right now. Doin' me a favor on their day off."

"Good! All right, we'll see you later." The apartment door closed.

He continued to tend to his plants; but he could not think about anything. In such a way do joy and misery, like opposing sine waves, cancel each other into a neutral blank.

Half an hour later, he went into the bathroom to check his face in the mirror. The puffiness was gone. The bright baby-blue shirt he had chosen to wear - now that he had no hothouse job to go to - brought out the blue of his eyes and generally improved his looks. He patted his belt with a secret pride that it was the same size as it was when he was twenty. Maybe he'd spend more time with Perce at the dojo. Work out. Get the serotonin flowing.

Beryl's door opened and two sets of footsteps descended the enclosed stairway. "Come on down!" he shouted like a Tv game host.

When Lilyanne reached the bottom she peeked around the wall as she used to in the hothouse. "Hello, George," she whispered.

"Hello, Peek a boo!"

She ran up to him and hugged him. "I think everything is going to be all right," she whispered in his ear; but when she pulled away, he could see her eyebrows were contracted. He admired the brave pretense, the consideration for others. "What a gal," he thought to himself.

He did not comment on her pain. "I think so, too. I'm relieved. Soon everything will be back to normal." Her hair was fluffy and smelled of Chanel perfume.

"Not quite," she said, releasing him. "Upstairs I called my mother. Can you believe that Henri is at my house already? He had breakfast with my mom and dad. My mom said that he was so anxious to see me that he'd wear dark glasses if it would make me feel better about my red eyes."

"Your eyes look fine, now," George said. "Just pink… not red."

"I showered upstairs and Beryl blow-dried my hair. I think I'll go home and have lunch with Henri. Beryl said she'd take me. He blames himself. He really does. He says he has a little surprise for me."

"Well, you mustn't keep the man waiting," George said.

The two women left by the kitchen door. When he was certain that they had gone, George put on a jacket and walked to the temple. Sensei wouldn't mind him sitting alone. The morning incense would have remained to give the meditation room the scent of sanctity. He wouldn't be disturbed. It was mandatory to turn cellphones off inside the temple.

Henri jumped down the portico steps to meet Lilyanne as she got out of the car. He picked her up and swung her around, "My angel!"

Beryl waved and proceeded down the drive as it curved around and headed back towards the entrance gate.

Henri had told Cecelia and Everett that as a joke he would place a new engagement ring in Lilyanne's glass of milk at the brunch that was waiting to be served. Everyone, except the countess who was noticeably absent, anticipated the moment Lilyanne would discover it.

She did not notice it during her first sip. But then she saw something dark move at the bottom of the glass. She picked up the glass again and squinted to see what it was. She lifted the glass high so that she could see the curved outline of the ring. "Aiiii," she squealed, "There's a ring in there!" And she hurriedly drank the glass of milk so that she could retrieve the ring. She let the ring slide into her mouth and held it between her teeth. With a great flourish, Henri took it and put it on her finger. The ring, a two carat diamond solitaire, sparkled in the sunlight.

It was a happy lunch. "Now," said Henri, "We really must talk about wedding plans!"

Tarleton House was, at last, a joyful place. The topics were all sources of joy. Bridal gowns. Masses. Churches. Receptions. Honeymoons. Titles. Residences. For the happy couple the future was bright.

Henri stayed for dinner. He could not bear to tear himself away from his beloved. Eric had dinner with the staff. He said little except that he had "never seen the guy so much in love. He's like a little kid."

At ten o'clock the lovers and the parents had worn themselves out expressing all their hopes and plans. This was the best day of their lives, they decided.

Henri kissed his beloved good night - and right in front of her parents! Lilyanne was embarrassed. Everyone laughed.

As Henri finally brought himself to release Lilyanne's hand, he got into the limo. "Since I'll be meeting your dad tomorrow at the country club for lunch, I won't be able to see you again until tomorrow evening," he said sorrowfully. He blew her a kiss. "So much to do," he said, "so much to do."

Everett beamed. He couldn't wait to show off his handsome future son-in-law to his friends.

THURSDAY, JANUARY 28, 2010

At seven o'clock in the morning, Eric inspected the array of images in the computer and congratulated Charlotte for having taken such masterful photographs.

"There is no substitute for experience," said Charlotte, "and now my work is done." She turned to Eric, "All set? Let's get me to the executive airport." As she walked out the door, she waved to Martin and Henri, "I'll see you all in the Caymans."

Henri jumped up and kissed her cheek. "Have a good flight, *Mamán*." Eric picked up her suitcases and the two left the suite.

Henri sat on a lounge chair and examined the photos in the laptop computer. He selected three photographs that he thought were particularly obscene and really did look as if Lilyanne were enjoying herself immensely. "Give me your opinion," he said. "Her cheeks were taped and pulled back a little… it looks like she's having an orgasm."

Martin squeezed down beside him "Yes," he whispered, "excellent." He scrolled through dozens of images. "Let's send them first."

Henri struck the command for the second-hand photo printer to reproduce the three images in 8 x 10 glossies.

"They're all great, " said Martin. "Next… how about these five? Henri ordered the photo printer to reproduce them.

"And the last group?" Martin asked. Henri again selected and printed the three photos.

They put latex gloves on and studied the eleven prints.

"How much should we demand first? 500K?" Henri asked.

"They're good for more."

"How is $600K?"

"$600K it is."

Henri selected an Italic font and began to type:

21 January, 2010

To Henri La Fontaine, Le Conte de Lisle,

My Brother In Honor,

I was presented with these scandalous photographs as if their only importance was to amuse me by their salaciousness. I was informed that the woman who is depicted in them has been living a double life. One life is of a proper and devout Catholic who is deserving of the honour of being a nobleman's wife. The gentleman who showed them to me said that he had heard today that you were that nobleman. Her other life, as is graphically displayed in these photographs, needs no additional word of description. When the gentleman learned that I was your friend, he said that he regretted that he had to mail them to various society editors and have them published in pornographic magazines. The notoriety, he insisted, would serve as a warning to the innocent.

When I protested, asking why he would take such a draconian action, he reminded me of an ancient injury your ancestors had done to his family and he wondered why he should do you any special favors.

I asked if honour had a price. He said he would get back to me; and he later called me and said that redemption is found in good works and in donations to those who did them. He (meaning you) could demonstrate his charitable nature by, say, donating the sum of $600,000. by end of business day January 29, 2010 Account #G140-3379-2156 Christian Eleemosynary Actions, Ltd. Ramparts Bank and Trust, George Town, Grand Cayman, Cayman Islands.

I am told that he personally supports several hospital and school ministries in Africa. I don't, however, know where they are located.

You will surely understand my need for anonymity.

We have known each other for many years. (A long school-mate friendship.)

I hope you will rethink your decision to marry this woman, if in fact that is or was your intention. Personally, I would ignore this request and let him do his damnedest.

If, however, there is an explanation for her behaviour... a temporary episode of some sort, then, of course, that is for you to decide.

Your old friend,
GTC.

Henri then began the second letter:

30 January, 2010
To Henri La Fontaine,
My dear friend,

How I wish I had not gotten involved in this sordid business.

This morning, by special messenger, I received these photographs and a note that said simply:

"Ramparts Bank has informed me that they did not receive your friend's donation by the January 29th deadline. Since your friend Henri did not comply with my request for a charitable donation, I can only deduce that despite the albeit brief announcement of his engagement to Miss Smith, either he is not interested in protecting her reputation or he is no longer interested in pursuing marriage with her.

Word has come to me that all of the buildings of two of the missions in Africa were destroyed and that considerable money is required to rebuild them and to pay off various officials.

I enclose 5 other photographs of this same woman and of her "clients." The donation I requested to be sent to the Cayman Islands account is therefore increased by $750,000. for a total of $1,350,000. by close of the work day February 5, 2010."

That was the message. I have no advice to offer you. I do believe that he seriously intends to have the photographs published.

Good luck with whichever course you decide to follow.

Your old friend,
GTC.

"Thank God the roads are clear," Henri said. "Another long drive for Eric to take to Princeton. Let's get the third letter typed so that we can get on with disposing of the laptop and the printer. Don't forget to do that flash drive memory thing of the photos."

"Yes, *Cher*, certainly."

Henri began to compose the third and final letter.

6 February 2010
To Henri La Fontaine.
Henri,

I resent more than I can say being used like this. I believe in Christian Charity. I also believe in wives and mothers who are respectable. And, frankly, I believe in the power of Redemption. But I do not know why I must be the middleman in this deplorable affair. This morning by messenger I received three more photographs and a message that stated that because (as I was told) you had deposited only six hundred thousand dollars in the Christian missions' account, your lady friend was far from redeemed.

Your wealth - and that it is mostly tied up in land and other property - is well known. I know that if you didn't send the full amount it was probably because such amounts must be gotten from liquidated assets. It isn't an easy matter to convert property into cash.

At any rate here are the photographs he sent. They are terrible. Just as I was preparing to mail this letter he called and said the mission rebuilding work in Africa is costing more than had been estimated. He wants to put an end to this business. I told him I was no longer available to be a "go-between." He said that he looked forward to receiving a donation that would provide the two million dollars total that between bricks and bribery the two missions now required.

I said I would write no more letters. He said that to ask for more would be unChristian. (his term, not mine). He reminded me that Redemption had to be uncomfortable... painful... or else there is no penance. Miss Smith should suffer for her immoralities. Send the additional donation - $750,000. and an additional $650,000. to the Cayman account. He will bother you and me no further. He has given me his assurance as a gentleman and a Christian *that this is the end of the photographs as far as he is concerned. If the money is made available, he says that he will go to Africa to observe personally the progress of the restoration. He truly believes that this charity does God's work in Africa.*

The deadline he gave is the 12th of February, 2010. On the 13th copies of all eleven photographs will be sent to your bride-to-be's family, country club, relatives, pastor, convent, society page editors, and to your mother and her relatives in Europe, and so on. I told him emphatically that this deadline was unreasonable and that he should give you a little more time. He said he would make his arrangements to return to Africa and give you the difference in time between the twelfth and whatever day it was his flight would leave.

All in all, two million dollars is a small price to pay to escape this kind of notoriety.

You will not hear from me again.

Goodbye old friend,
GTC.

Henri printed the letters and grouped them with three piles of photographs. He took the first manila envelope that contained a few paper bags and had already been received at the hotel desk, opened it with a letter knife, removed the bags, and with bare hands, he inserted the first letter dated January 21st, and the first group of photographs. The envelope, however, now bore his fingerprints as well as those of the postal employees, hotel personnel, and Martin's. He wrinkled the envelope so that the photographs inside would look as though they had gone through normal handling.

Martin, wearing gloves, printed Henri's name and hotel address on the second envelope and inserted the letter dated January 30th and the batch of five photographs into it. He sealed it with distilled water and put it into a separate plastic bag for Eric to take to Princeton to mail as soon as he returned from the airport.

He repeated this for the third letter and three photographs and put the envelope into his suitcase to await the next mailing. Martin took a screwdriver and meticulously began to take apart the printer and the computer, preparing to discard them in pieces.

Henri looked at his watch and calculated the time in Austria. He had plenty of time to reach his banker in Vienna. Using the hotel phone, he asked the receptionist to place a call to his banker in Vienna and to announce his call. Whenever the operator was on the line, a red light appeared on the phone. When she closed the connection, the light went out and he knew he could speak privately. When his banker was on the line Henri asked that six hundred thousand dollars be transferred into the Christian Eleemosynary Actions' account in the Cayman Islands as a charitable contribution. His banker asked him to confirm this in his own hand by fax. The request should also have an appropriate cover letter. "The Cayman Islands Monetary Authority has just instituted new regulations," he explained. "There are tighter controls. Transfer agencies are now verifying sources. We've entered a new era of terrorism, money laundering, drugs, illegal weapon sales, dictators looting their own treasuries, and so on. It's not the old bribery, fraud, and embezzlement money any more. The CIMA is finally putting the onus of determining the legitimacy of money transfers on the sender." He sighed. "I'll do my best and fax whatever additional forms the transfer requires. That's the best I can do."

"One more thing," Henri said. "If another banker or official of some kind asks you whether this sum was transferred from my account, tell him that it was and if he presses, tell him where it was transferred to. You've done this before for me. Don't tell anyone I gave you instructions to reveal this. Ah, I know I can count on your discretion. Sometimes people with whom one does business like to be sure that one's word is truthful. And you can also verify that my mother has withdrawn funds from my account - should the subject come up."

Henri rubbed hand lotion onto his face, making sure enough of it got into his eyes to irritate them. Affecting a harried expression, he went down to the manager's office and asked him and his secretary to witness his signature and then to fax two documents to Austria and to be prepared to receive faxes from the same country.

Bad news infested Tarleton House less than twelve hours after they decided that Wednesday had been the most carefree day of their lives. The jeweler called to tell Cecelia that replacing the stones could possibly cost "about half a million dollars, maybe more." He read the list of fake stones and the approximate cost of their authentic replacements. He emailed a scanned photograph of the pieces which marked the false stones in red Xs.

"What does 'maybe more' mean?" Cecelia asked.

"No one keeps such a variety of stones of this quality and size on hand. I am not designing a new necklace. There are five pieces: The stones in the two earrings must perfectly match! The tiara, necklace and bracelet have lost many stones and I must find replacements that not only are similarly cut but precisely fit the existing settings! I will need to make careful measurements before I search the market for all that is needed. Until I know the cost of each stone, I can give only a rough estimate. When your insurance company contacts me, I'll give them a detailed analysis of the loss. I trust you've filed a police report."

"No! We will absorb the loss ourselves. We do not want police bunglers interfering in this tragic event. My daughter had just gotten engaged. Her engagement ring was also stolen. Her fiancé is a member of the aristocracy. Just replace the stones with as little notoriety as possible."

Shaken, she called Jake Kaslan, their broker, to order that he sell 1.5 million dollars worth of their securities and to transfer the funds to their bank. Kaslan faxed the order to her and she and Everett signed it. "We'll have some extra funds at the ready… for the wedding's incidentals," she explained. Yes, the wedding. A color scheme for the flowers at the church. Calling the Contesse to ask for her opinion would be a congenial gesture. Perhaps their family had a traditional color or choice of flower. It would be an antidote to that wretched jewelry business. She called the hotel and asked for the Contesse deLisle. "Oh, Madam has left the hotel," the telephone receptionist said.

"Left?" asked Cecelia in complete confusion. "Where did she go?"

"I'm sorry but I don't have that information," the girl replied. "Do you wish me to ring her suite?"

"Yes. I'll speak to Henri LaFontaine."

"Very good, Madam."

The line clicked and Martin answered the phone. Apprehensively, Cecelia Smith gave her name and asked if Henri LaFontaine was there.

"His Lordship has gone out unexpectedly," said Martin. "I regret that I do not know the time of his return. May I have him call you?"

"When is the Countess deLisle expected to return?"

"I don't think we have a specific time. It may be a few days. I cannot say."

"Then," Cecelia replied nervously, "please have his Lordship call me as soon as it is convenient."

Anxiety had tightened her chest. Was this an indication that Henri and his mother were beginning to withdraw from the engagement? She decided not to discuss with Lilyanne the cost of repairing the jewelry or to tell her that the Contesse had left town. "Who knows what that twit will say or do in response."

As soon as he arrived in Princeton, Eric parked at the outer edge of a mall, which was located two blocks from a post office. Wearing casual clothing, he walked to the mailbox outside the post office and deposited the manila envelope. Then he calmly walked back to the car and began his drive back to Philadelphia.

Everett, after boasting about his handsome, titled, young, soon-to-be son-in-law, considered calling home to find out if there was some reason why Henri was now forty-five minutes late. No, he decided, that would make him seem too anxious. He would relax - or at least appear to be relaxed - and continue to answer all inquiries about the vaunted guest: "These lovers…. time means nothing to them. What can we do? It's the same all over the world."

At one thirty he summoned his driver and returned to Tarleton House.

He marched up the front steps and, being met by his wife, demanded that she explain such unconscionable behavior. "What the hell is going on?"

Cecelia could say only that she was as mystified as he. She had tried to reach Henri but he was out and the valet didn't know when he'd be back."

"Call him again," Everett demanded.

"You call him!" she countered.

Everett tried Henri's cellphone which went immediately to voicemail. He called the hotel desk and was again told by Henri's valet that he did not know when his Lordship would return; but that he would give him the message that Mr. Everett Smith had called.

Eric returned to the hotel parking lot having settled in his mind a subject that had plagued him all the way back from Princeton. He was hungry, and he would have filet mignon for a late lunch.

He let himself into the suite and, hearing Martin and Henri spashing in the tub, went directly into the bathroom. "Have you two eaten?" He asked.

"No," said Martin. "We were waiting for you. How did it go?"

"No problem. The road was good, there and back. So, bring me up to speed," Eric said as he began to urinate.

Martin got out of the tub first. "Her father called. He wants to talk to Henri."

As Martin called room service and ordered early dinner for three, Everett Smith, having waited impatiently for nearly an hour, again called the hotel and asked to be connected to Henri La Fontaine. The receptionist said the line was in use. Did he want to wait? No, he did not. He hung up and shouted at Cecelia, "Who does that son of a bitch think he is? He made a fool out of me at the club. And not so much as a god damned phone call!"

"That's right, you idiot," she answered. "Blow off some more steam so that you'll have something else to apologize for when you do receive an explanation. Wait another half hour and then we'll call again."

After they had eaten, it was time to make the first "notification" call.

Martin and Eric knew to be absolutely quiet as Henri called Tarleton House and asked in a shaky voice to speak to Everett Smith.

Everett, not knowing why he had been stood up at lunch and had not received so much as a phone call, answered in as neutral a tone as he could manage. "This is Everett Smith."

Henri stuttered and paused and slightly whined, "Th.. this is Henri. Lilyanne's be.. be.. betrothed."

"You sound terrible. Where are you?"

"I'm… here… I'm at the… the hotel. I couldn't meet… you for.. for lunch. Something… something ter.. terrible has happened." Suddenly his voice was firm and pleading. "Do not tell your wife or my fiancee what I am telling you now." He sucked in air violently. Then he took a deep breath and resumed his shaky voice. "I… I don't think I.. I.. should tell you … tell you over the ph.. phone. Pick a.. a.. place… between here and… and where you are. I'll leave now."

"There's a Lieutenant Long's Inn in Broomall. I'll meet you there." He hung up and announced that this was as far as he was willing to go with the whole business.

An hour later, two limousines, coming from different directions, pulled into the parking lot of the Inn.

Everett, looking like a man who had just realized that his wallet had been stolen, walked to Henri's limousine. Henri, who had put hand lotion in his eyes again so that they were extremely red and irritated and had started to swell from having been rubbed for twenty miles, took a small carrying case with him and got out of the car without waiting for Eric to open the door.

"Will we have privacy in there?" Henri asked Everett.

"Yes. What is this all about?"

Henri did not answer but walked straight into the restaurant section of the Inn. Everett followed and told the seating hostess to put them in as private a table as possible.

Everett ordered two scotch and sodas as Henri began to remove documents from the case.

When the drinks arrived, Everett said to the waiter, "We'll call you when we need anything more." Then he said to Henri, "All right, let's have it."

Henri hesitated and then gave him the letter dated January 21st. "It came yesterday but I didn't get home from your house until late. So I didn't look at my mail until this morning."

Everett read the letter. "What does this mean?" Henri pushed the envelope across the table and put his hands over his face. He did not see Everett's wide-eyed expression of horror as he gasped, "There must be some mistake! These photographes have got to be faked somehow. Photoshopped."

"I know that and you know that but the fact is that they have been faked so well that not even the one expert I dared to have look at them could detect any trickery. I just cannot go around asking strangers to see if these are genuine photographs. I had my driver take them into a photography shop - some man he met when he was off duty having a drink in a bar. If you know of an expert who is discreet… absolutely discreet… have him examine them." He took out his handkerchief and wiped his eyes.

Everett was still in a state of shock. His hands trembled as he held the photographs. "What do you propose to do about the blackmail? And make no mistake, this is blackmail."

"I paid it! What did you think I would do? Risk having anyone see these even if they are fakes!" He placed the two faxed documents on the table. "I had my banker wire $600,000. to the Cayman Islands. My God. My God. Why would any beast do this to my angel? Is this how God repays goodness and piety? Is He determined to martyr her into some kind of sainthood? My God. My God." He began to sob. His body shook and his cheeks were flooded with tears. He could not speak for five minutes.

While Henri wept, Everett studied the photographs. Lilyanne's face and naked body were as exposed as possible, but the men she was photographed with could not be seen face-front. In profile, they appeared to be four different men. The quality of the photos was also different.

Some pictures were grainier than others. There was no question of her head being photoshopped onto someone else's body. Her scars were unmistakable. Both body and face were clearly hers. But there was still a slim possibility that the photos had been manipulated. "I'd like to look for trickery in the photographs.. I'd need to see them under a magnifying glass. May I take these and examine them more closely?" he asked.

"Only on condition that you do not show them to Lilyanne or, I would also prefer, to your wife. Now you see why my dear mother hired a private detective. People hate aristocrats. They would do anything to drag us into their slime. If these are legitimate photographs then I know that Lilyanne was drugged... or hypnotized... something!" He wiped his eyes and blew his nose. "I am devastated by this... but," he grew defiant, "they will not win. Remember, I can take Lilyanne to... to Fiji! If this filth is ever circulated I will not allow her to be harmed. I will take her away to wherever she wants to go." He stood up and said, "I have to go. I'm feeling nauseous. I've been trying to cope with this problem all day."

"Did your mother see these?" Everett asked.

Henri made a slight retching noise and put his handkerchief to his mouth. "Yes. I gasped when I opened the envelope. She was standing nearby and pulled one of the photographs out of my hands. She insisted on seeing the others. I assured her they were fake... but she doesn't want to deal with truth! It's always the appearance of things that counts. She went to the airport... I don't know where she went. Probably to stay with friends in Virginia. I don't know and I don't care. I'll call you tomorrow. Please give my apologies to your wife and precious daughter. I don't want to talk to anyone until I'm composed. Make up any excuse you like." He hurried out of the restaurant.

Everett Smith sat at the table and stared at the manila envelope, the blackmail letter, the photographs, the faxed letters. He saw that the envelope had been mailed from Princeton. He saw the initials GTC. He should have asked Henri if he knew what they stood for. He saw the fax cover letter and the manager's signature from the hotel. He thought he knew the manager's name.... Middleton... from somewhere, but he couldn't remember. He would call his banker and ask if the bank and the transfer agent were legitimate. He put all the papers and photos inside the envelope.

Everett tried to think constructively all the way home. He would reimburse Henri. Why should the boy have to pay. It isn't as if they were already married. He had to tell Cecelia about the photographs. But he didn't have to tell her he was reimbursing Henri. He and Cecelia had a special joint account with the broker. No order to buy or sell could be made unilaterally. But he did have one old account that was his alone. He could cover the 600K.

And yes, there was a possibility that this was an elaborate hoax, a fraud. The actions in the photographs were not genuine, perhaps the principals were not genuine, either.

At home, he went into his study and locked the door. He needed to think. The photographs were emotional poison and only the 'antidote of rational thought' could neutralize their effect. All right, he would verify the story as much as possible.

The faxed authorizations had been made in the General Manager's office of The Declan hotel. Smith summoned his *major domo* to his study. "Sanford, do we know a John Middleton who is the general manager of The Declan? I recall the name, but I just can't place it."

Sanford recalled that there was a John Middleton who had won the Inter-Country Club golf tournament several years before. "Did he play for my club?" Smith asked.

"I don't believe so, but I can find out. Would you like me to?" Sanford got out his smart phone. He called the pro-shop of Everett's Club. He asked, listened, and thanked the salesman. "Middleton of Manufacturer's won in 2007," he said, to which Smith raised his eyebrows. It was an expensive club to join. Everett Smith adjusted his attitude and called John Middleton.

"John," he said warmly, "this is Everett Smith, one of the men who are still chaffing about your victory on the links a couple of years ago. How are you or more to the point, how are the greens treating you?"

"Ev, old man, are you still a sore loser? Maybe we can arrange a few mulligans for you next time we tee off."

The stage having been set, Smith explained the impending marriage situation and a father's natural inclination to know if everything underneath was as it appeared on the surface. Middleton verified his notary seal on the document and said that as far as he could tell, the guests were exactly what they appeared to be. But he'd keep his "eye on the ball."

Smith next called a friend of his in the Department of State in Washington whose particular area of expertise was Germany and Austria. "I don't want you to betray any state secrets," said Everett, "I'm just looking for some social verifications. Have you ever heard of the Countess deLisle and Henri La Fontaine?"

"Charlotte? Sure I know her. I saw Henri once.. years ago when he was a teen ager. She was a beauty then… she's still extremely attractive."

"What I want to know is are they the real McCoy?"

"They rent out a house they own in Vienna so they're not in town much. I don't verify every French nobleman's name or his right to use that title. Ever since Napoleon, titles have become meaningless. I'm sure the deLisle name is an old one, and I've no reason to doubt that Charlotte's husband had a right to it; but beyond that I can't verify anything."

"Are they rich and socially acceptable?" Everett insisted.

"If being invited to Embassy parties in D.C. and the Court of Saint James are indications, I'd say they were socially acceptable, and judging from the jewelry I've seen her wear, rich, too."

Everett thanked his friend and called his banker, Brent Bache. With his voice registering parental concern, he conveyed to the banker the importance of his request, asked him to verify the existence of the Austrian bank, Henri's account, the banker and agent who made the $600,000. transfer, and also the Cayman Islands account. The banker said that he would try to get the information - which might not be easy or even possible - but he'd do his best and would call back within the hour. It was late, but Bache could hear the tension in his friend's voice.

"I may have to get up in the middle of the night to reach Vienna in their morning, but I'll do it. Stay relaxed, Ev."

Everett called his wife into his study and asked her to sit down. He told her everything and said that he was waiting on a final call-back to verify the authenticity of the Vienna transaction. "If everything is as it is alleged to be, we have been blessed with one gracious son-in-law." Then he showed her the photographs. Cecelia Smith went limp and fainted, falling forward from the chair onto the floor. Everett summoned Sanford and asked him to bring ammonia smelling salts to his study.

When Cecelia regained consciousness, the two men helped her to rest on the couch; and when they were alone again, Cecelia asked her husband to bring her the photographs. She studied the three pictures and began to moan and speak incoherently. Everett kept repeating, "They're fakes. They're obviously fakes." She did not hear him. When she finally stopped crying and sat exhausted on the couch, she said, "I knew that sooner or later that little ingrate would ruin everything." She had to be helped to her bed.

Cecelia promised not to tell Lilyanne anything about the photos. The promise required no effort to keep. She announced to the chambermaid that she had a blinding migraine headache and under no circumstance was she to be disturbed… by anyone.

At dinner, Lilyane asked her father why she hadn't heard from Henri. "But you did hear from him," Everett said, "through me. I had a few drinks with him in Broomall. We both got our signals crossed and wound up having to compromise on Lieutenant Long's Inn. He looks good and is in wonderful spirits thinking about his angel. He's got a million things to do. Be patient. He'll call tomorrow, I'm sure."

FRIDAY, JANUARY 29, 2010

Beryl sat back in her desk chair and wondered how many loose ends she hadn't tied. While it was true that they were no longer contracted to investigate anything, George - like it or not - was involved in this mystery. She wanted to know more about the moment in time that George got involved in Lilyanne's abduction. She took James Barton's business card from her purse. She would start by calling him.

"I just have a few questions," she said apologetically. "What precisely was taking place when the card was handed to Lilyanne? Start with leaving the box and try to be as precise as possible." She clicked on a pen and began to take notes.

James thought for a moment. "Precisely? We four left the box to go out into the mezzanine for the second intermission. There were many people on the floor... milling about.... some headed for the bar or the toilets. I turned to Felice to ask her how she was holding up under the strain. Those were my exact words - the opera is very long. She said her girdle was killing her. I looked around and didn't see Henri or Lilyanne.

"I turned and asked Felice if she wanted something from the bar. She said, 'Yes, a transfusion.' I laughed and whispered in her ear that if she preferred, I'd help her with her girdle. 'Right here?' she said. I put my arm around her and kissed her on her neck... we were laughing... and then I headed for the bar. I saw Henri coming back with both hands full, carrying two champagne cocktails. I kept on going to the bar. I got two cocktails and went back. I gave one to Felice. I didn't see Lilyanne but figured she had gone to the ladies room. I asked Henri if he had seen the Ring in Europe. I specifically asked if he had seen it at Wagner's opera house in Bayreuth. He said his mother and the Wagner family were personal friends. He said they saw the Ring often. He named some of the places with alliteration... let me get this straight... Sydney and Seattle, London and Los Angeles.. and some other place. I said, 'You must really like it.' And he answered, 'Ever since I learned to sleep with my eyes open and my ears closed' - or words to that effect - 'I really love it.' And we laughed. Felice wanted to know what we were giggling about. But at that same time I asked Henri, *sotto voce*, if he ever heard Mark Twain's line, "Wagner's music is not as bad as it sounds" and he said he had - but then he countered with something Rossini said... "Wagner's music has beautiful minutes and awful half hours," I hadn't heard it so we laughed and Felice kept tugging my arm asking me what was so funny. I told her and the three of us laughed, and when I looked around I saw Lilyanne talking to an usher. She had a white business card in her hand. We were still laughing. We had our heads together because, naturally, we didn't want anyone to hear us dissing Wagner. When I looked again she was gone. You know the rest."

Nothing stood out; but a least she had a fresh image of the moment George's card was used to lure Lilyanne outside. She thanked him and asked him to give her a call if he remembered anything else. As she ended the call, the alliteration kept repeating in her mind...."Sydney and Seattle, London and Los Angeles."

When the banker called to verify that all the accounts were legitimate and in good order, Smith thanked him and added, "I may be asking you to transfer a large sum of money to the Austrian account. I'll keep in touch."

After lunch Henri called and asked for Lilyanne. Sanford found her in the hothouse and told her Henri was waiting for her on the phone. She ran to the house and breathlessly answered.

"Hello, Angel Girl! I still don't have transportation - they didn't have the car finished as they said they would."

Lilyanne was disappointed. Henri asked if her father would be willing to send his car into town to get him... or, better yet, would he send her into town and they could have dinner and go to the movies.

Lilyanne asked him to hold on, "I'll go ask him now," she said. She ran to the study and knocked on the door. Everett refused to open it. "What is it?" he asked. She told him Henri was having car trouble and wanted her to come into town for dinner and a movie. Could she be driven there by their driver?

Everett had just finished an argument with his wife. He could tolerate no more social strains. "No, I'm sorry," he said. "I need the car myself this afternoon... all day, in fact. Tell him to call you again tomorrow." Everett Smith's eyes were red and his face was bloated. He needed to be left alone.

She couldn't conceal her disappointment. Her eyes filled with tears. "Daddy says he needs the car this afternoon. Can you call again tomorrow?"

Henri told her he loved her and would call her again Saturday morning.

She returned to the hothouse. Sanford waited fifteen minutes then found an excuse to go to join her. She was crying, holding one of the Monja Blanca plants in her arms. Sanford went up to her and took the plant from her. He placed it on the table, then he put his arm around her shoulder. "It's all right, Miss Lilyanne. Go ahead and cry." She began to cry softly, whimpering as she let her head rest against his chest. "Oh, Sanford, when this week started I thought I was the happiest woman in the world. But this week has been a nightmare. I'm so scared."

Sanford began to think that if things didn't get better, he ought to talk to George Wagner. Sanford had heard the strange crying and shouting in the house all week. The jewelry removal. The nights Lilyanne wasn't home. The blotches on her face when she did return. The missed lunch date at the club. The smelling salts. It made no sense. And now this refusal to let her use the car. He knew that Everett Smith had no plans to go out on Friday afternoon or evening. The car was available. Something was very wrong.

On their way to Northeast Philadelphia Airport, Charlotte changed her clothes in the limo. She put on slacks, shirt, camping jacket, and replaced her high heels with socks and tennis shoes. She changed her jewelry to Native American turquoise and silver and her purse to a leather shoulder bag. Eric stopped at a gas station and she went in to the ladies room to complete the change in appearance.

She first took the hair pins out of her hair and then combed and wet it, letting it hang down to her shoulders. She wore large sun glasses and a hat that had a wired brim she could bend and adjust as a sun shield. She now looked like an entirely different woman, Beatrix van Aken from Suriname. She carried a Suriname passport, pilot's license, and all other necessary documentation including an assortment of credit cards in that name. She also carried a notarized lease agreement for the Piper which named Charlotte as lessor and Beatrix as lessee.

She planned to fly to Tampa, Florida, then to Cancun, Mexico, and then to the Caymans. She filed a flight plan listing her destination as General Aviation Terminal, Owen Roberts Airport, George Town, Grand Cayman Island. Michel had bought her a 1980 Piper Dakota which she kept in mint condition. In nearly thirty years, it was either in the air or inside a hangar.

She had taken care of all airport fees, including the mechanic's bill for the engine tune up, and ready now to begin her flight, she started the engine and waved goodbye to Eric who waited until she was safely airborne before he drove away.

Michel had introduced her to the writings of Carl Jung; and in Jung's autobiography she learned that he could conjure up a kind of ghost, an archetypal ghost-friend he called Philemon who was so real that Jung could stroll through his garden having long rewarding talks with him. She also read Alexandra David-Neel's account of her experiences in Tibet. This intrepid descendant of the artist David, had acquired, through disciplined meditation, the ability to conjure up a fat jolly monk who would be her companion during the long days she was alone in her hut.

Wanting to acquire that ability for herself, Charlotte found an old yogi who instructed her to concentrate with great deliberation, "As an actor rehearses his part so thoroughly that he becomes the character he portrays, and the play is not a drama being performed before an audience, but an event in his own life." He had warned her that if the actor would then break his concentration and would begin to think of his ego-self and the presence of other actors on the stage or on the critical observers in the audience, he would forget his lines and become confused and end his existence in art's reality.

On these long solo flights she would practice the method the yogi taught her. She would concentrate fiercely and then conjure up a confidante and mentor who would tell her how beautiful and noble she was. He would wax eloquent about the satisfactions and joys that could be had by helping those who were born into a life of suffering. And then, when she landed in the Cayman Islands and ceased to be the island-hopping Beatrix Van Aken and would morph into the old-fashioned and timid Mrs. Harriet Williams, resident agent of the Christian Eleemosynary Actions, Ltd., she would repeat those noble sentiments whenever she spoke about the work the CEA was doing to aid the unfortunate poor of Africa.

Henri called Lilyanne. Sanford quietly went to tell her he was calling. He switched the call to the kitchen and she talked to him there. The cook sent everyone, including the housekeeper, into the pantry so that she could speak privately.

Henri was excited. "What about tonight? Can you come out? I have the car... finally!"

The coldness that had been confronting her at home made her eager for the date. "Yes," she said. "Of course! What should I wear?"

"Do you want to have dinner first?"

"Yes, that would be lovely."

"Well, let's not go formal or in dressy clothes. Wear a blouse and slacks and we can eat in a less formal dining room. I'm tired of rich food. I'd like to eat more simple fare for a change. How about you?"

"I have a new outfit that will be perfect. What time should I be ready?"

"I'll come by at… say… 4:30."

"Wonderful. I'll be ready."

Lilyanne ran up to her bedroom and took a quick shower and dressed. She knocked on the door to Everett's study. "Daddy, I'm going out with Henri." Then she ran outside and was standing on the portico as the cream colored limo came up the driveway.

Everett left his self-imposed seclusion to stand beside his daughter on the portico.

The car pulled up and Henri jumped out to catch Lilyanne as she jumped from the bottom step. He swung her around. "Everett!" he called with one arm around Lilyanne and the other extended to shake hands with Everett.

The older man took his hand. "I didn't know you'd be here. Come in!"

"We were going out for something to eat and then maybe take in a film," Henri explained. "As you can see, it's strictly informal. Why don't you join us. Is there a good place to eat around here?"

"My club," said Everett, anxious to eradicate the embarrassment he felt by the aborted lunch date. "We've got an informal dining room for the folks who've been exercising. The food is excellent."

"Then that's good enough," Henri said, "if, of course, it is ok with my bride-to-be."

"Yes! Yes! Let's go! Come on, Daddy. You can come just as you are."

"Let me call ahead and make a reservation," said Everett. He went back into his study, called the club and was told the reservation list was full. Hearing the "or else" threat in his voice, the club agreed to accommodate the party. Everett quickly brushed his teeth and removed some stubble with his electric razor. He slapped water onto his face, tucked his casual shirt into his pants, and pulled on a heavy sweater.

In minutes, he was sitting with his daughter and future son-in-law, for whom he felt more affection now that he had verified the actions Henri had taken to prevent Lilyanne's name from being scandalized.

Cecelia Smith looked down from her bedroom window and watched the happy scene. So they were going out without her - without even bothering to consult or invite her. For all she knew her daughter would once again succumb to stupidity and bring more grief upon her. The more she thought about it, the more incensed she became. Finally, at the same time that the miscreant diners were being ushered to their table, Cecelia Tarleton Smith picked up the phone, called the caretaker of her summer home in Cape May, New Jersey, and told him to recall the housekeeper, cook, and maid who all lived locally, and to order all the utilities to be turned on immediately, regardless of any additional expense. Everything should be prepared to receive her within the few hours that it took for her to be driven there. Then she hastily packed a bag of warm clothing, and feeling too nervous and too groggy to drive herself, summoned the chauffeur, and left the house.

SUNDAY, JANUARY 31, 2010

Beryl, George, and Sensei decided to go out for brunch after services. It was Beryl's idea. George had been seriously depressed since she had taken Lilyanne home on Wednesday. He saw his physician again who told him to look for the silver lining, get a hobby, meet some new people, cultivate a positive attitude and not get started on mood altering drugs. But George wore his sadness like a suit of armor. It was impervious to the platitudes and pep talks hurled against it. Inside his defensive shield, he felt old. His arm ached. His knee ached. He lost his appetite. Even the Monja Blanca orchid that he had brought home from the Smith collection and kept on his kitchen table discomfited him whenever he looked at it. It was a young plant and he expected that it would die before it ever bloomed.

Sunday morning he awakened feeling an urgent need to get rid of the metal tables, racks, and bolted steel shelves that filled his living and dining rooms and the room he had used as his office. He decided to bring back the furniture that he and Beryl had put in the garage to make room for all the orchid plants. He would put all the tables, racks, and shelves out at the curb on trash day. Passers by would probably take them before the garbage truck arrived. The plants they once held were safe at the Eckersley estate and he had no intention of bringing them back.

The rooms looked so pathetic now. Without curtains or drapes on the windows, the light was harsh and amplified the ugliness. The wall to wall carpet was filthy. It embarrassed him to imagine what Lilyanne must have thought when she saw the bizarre way he lived. Yes, he'd restore the rooms to the way they used to look. Most of the furniture was in a rustic, colonial style, which his wife thought was more "homey" for children. He had also emptied a small office to make room for the plants. The furniture that had been in there was in a modern style that he much preferred.

He opened the garage door and was shocked to see the condition of the pieces. He had remembered them as they were when they first furnished his home… when the kids hid their toys under the couch and his wife fluffed up the pillows and leveled the lampshades. Now they looked shabby, faded, and stained. They smelled moldy. For all he knew they were full of roaches and other vermin.

He returned to the living room and looked at the rug. He remembered when his wife would vacuum it and leave ridges in the pile or walk across the room and stop suddenly to pick up a little piece of lint or paper. Now the rug was filled with matted clumps of spilled orchid soil and water stains.

He always liked the way Beryl's apartment looked. He liked the Zen Temple, too. Maybe he would hire the contractor who did Beryl's apartment and have the place completely done over in the Japanese style. While the work was being done he'd go down to Florida to visit his brother for a few weeks. This was the only solution he could think of that might help him to escape from his armor plated stasis - this, and not having to return to the embarrassing state of his house.

He decided that the very next morning, when the contractor's office was open, he'd call and initiate the transformation.

Henri and Eric returned to Martin at the Declan late in the evening Saturday night. Henri, quoting Henley, thanked "whatever gods there be for my unconquerable soul." Eric was famished. The three had a late celebration just before the kitchen closed. Wine and chateaubriand with sauce Bernaise; crisp fried slices of steamed potatoes; asparagus spears; and creme brulée for dessert. And three $200.00 bottles of burgundy.

"*A la media luna,*" said Martin, raising his glass, "two more weeks to go. The beach is calling!" They ate and drank until three in the morning and slept until noon.

Henri consulted the hotel visitors' brochure and found the name of the nearest Catholic church and the hours the Mass was celebrated. Then he called Lilyanne and told her he had gone to Mass locally because, as he put it, he regarded it as his duty as an employer to see to it that his servants did not neglect their spiritual duties.

He whispered that it embarrassed them to go in their uniforms... chauffeur and valet.. so he allowed them to dress respectably in civilian garments, and he hoped that she would not object to the practice when they were married.

Lilyanne saw Henri as a true Defender of the Faith. They spoke for half an hour and then he told her that he had several calls to make. He told her that he would see her for lunch the next day. He gave her a kiss on the phone and told her he loved her. She giggled and said she loved him, too. And then she ran to tell her father how Henri took his servants to Mass.

Everett had just called Cape May, New Jersey, to ask his wife when his car and driver would be returned, when Lilyanne burst into his study to tell him about Henri's concern for the spiritual state of his employees. Everett Smith conveyed the hagiographic data to his wife.

"Has his mother returned?" she asked.

"Not that I know of," Everett replied.

"I will remain here," she said, "away from the travesty. Let the circus go on without either of us. I'll send the car back to Tarleton."

Cecelia was humiliated to think that someone had had the audacity to investigate the Tarleton-Smith family! And then to pass muster only to have this disaster occur! Why hadn't that stupid Wagner discovered what her daughter was up to? He was an incompetent fool. And now her husband wanted to canonize the son of that ridiculous countess. He was supposed to be a saint because he paid off blackmailers. How often in her life would she be confronted with such images of her daughter's debauchery? How long before the Contesse openly ridiculed her daughter-in-law? The world would ridicule the Smith family. How could she ever show her face again in public. Why did her beautiful boy have to die? What did she, Cecelia Tarleton Smith, ever do to deserve this?

MONDAY, FEBRUARY 1, 2010

Henri called Lilyanne and talked about wedding gowns. She wanted to know if he liked full skirts. He didn't. He preferred a simple dress with a short veil. No train... no stable full of attendants. But naturally he would love anything she chose.

"My mother will be back from Cape May tomorrow, I think," she said. "We'll go shopping for a dress. I'm so glad you told me what you like. I want to look nice for you."

They talked about honeymoons. He had been all over the world. She had been nowhere. What did he like? "This time of year Tobago is nice," he said, "especially when we can rent a private cottage on the beach."

"Oh, I'd love that. I'm going to look up Tobago on the Internet and see pictures. You are the most wonderful man in the world. God has been so good to me."

George called Beryl's Japanese decorator and made an appointment. "I'm meeting him tomorrow morning, so I won't be coming in," he said to Beryl. "Can you cover for me?"

"I'm glad to see you're shaking yourself free of that love cement you were getting stuck in. I hope you like the result," she said. "You need the change. But it's such a big house for a bachelor. Have you ever considered getting a new place?"

"Never. For some crazy reason I keep thinking that if my kids ever want to come home, they'll know where to find it."

TUESDAY, FEBRUARY 2, 2010

John Middleton, Manager of the Declan Hotel, whose interest in Henri La Fontaine had been piqued by Everett Smith's inquiries, began personally to look through the mail when it arrived each early afternoon. He also asked the clerks, waiters and chambermaids to keep their ears open whenever they were in the Countess's suite and report to him anything that seemed unusual.

On Tuesday, another large manila envelope arrived, addressed to Henri. It had been postmarked in Princeton, New Jersey, and bore no return address. At 1 p.m. as was his custom, the young nobleman's valet came to the desk to collect the mail. He nodded a greeting to the clerk and returned to the suite.

Fifteen minutes later, the telephone operator answered a request from Henri LaFontaine to place a call to Vienna and to announce his call. There was no answer except a recording of the bank's hours.

The receptionist reported to John Middleton that "Mr. La Fontaine seemed to be agitated." Middleton didn't know if this were significant or not. To learn more, he asked the kitchen to prepare a small fruit basket which he kept on his desk in case another mysterious call was placed. In another fifteen minutes she signaled him that an overseas call was being made. Middleton asked her to be slow to respond to the request. Immediately he instructed a waiter to take the fruit basket to the suite as a 'complimentary gift' along with a small bowl of yogurt, plates, utensils and napkins, and to "keep his ears open."

The call was to the Ramparts Bank and Trust, George Town, Grand Cayman Island.

The waiter returned to report that the bank had apparently refused to provide any information. "Mr. La Fontaine was furious," the waiter said. "He demanded to know why a six-hundred thousand dollar deposit had not been credited to his account on or before the 29th of January. He began to shout, 'What kind of incompetent fools are you that this was not done efficiently?' The person he was speaking to refused to give him any information and La Fontaine demanded general information about a Christian Charity group. 'Are you sure these are legitimate people? Do you know them? Have you seen them with your own eyes?' Apparently the bank said that they were local and reputable people." That was all the waiter could overhear.

John Middleton did not know what this meant, either. But he thought he should call Everett to tell him. Everett Smith was relieved to learn that it was clearly evident that La Fontaine did not know who the recipients of the blackmail were.

As he concluded his call with Everett Smith, he looked up to see Henri La Fontaine standing in his office doorway.

Clearly agitated, La Fontaine asked for a set of faxed instructions and authorizations be sent to the same bank in Vienna, but this time the amount was for $750,000. The payee was the same Christian charity in the Cayman Islands.

John Middleton called Everett Smith to tell him about this ominous development. Smith thanked him and found it ironic to be thanking a man for having pushed him down into one of the Inferno's deepest circles. He couldn't remember which circle was reserved for bribe and blackmail payers.

WEDNESDAY, FEBRUARY 3, 2010

Faxed messages from Vienna were waiting for John Middleton when he came to his office Wednesday morning. The messages were to be delivered to Henri La Fontaine, but Middleton naturally read them. The banker in Austria regretted that La Contesse had removed all but twenty thousand euros from his account. He could not comply with the request to transfer $750,000. to the charity account in the Cayman Islands.

Middleton knew that it was early, but felt that the young nobleman should receive the communications immediately and that he should deliver them to him, himself. He put the faxed documents in an envelope and carried them to the door of the addressee.

La Fontaine answered the door himself. He was fully dressed and had rosary beads in his hand when he accepted the envelope and in an absent-minded way, indicated that Middleton should enter the suite.

"The news," Middleton would later report to Everett Smith, "caused his Lordship to sink to his knees and tremble. He kept repeating, 'It can't be! How could she do this to me?' Over and over he repeated this. He went into the bathroom. Clearly he did not want me to see him crying. But his eyes were tearful. He was devastated."

Everett Smith's tenure in the Inferno was extended. "You're a good friend, John," he said. "Please continue to keep me in the loop. I'm in your debt and I won't forget your kindness."

Henri La Fontaine sat on his bed and flipped the pages of an address book. "I think that three or four ought to be enough," he said to Martin Williams Shannon. "I'll call Mexico City first."

Affecting agitation, he asked the receptionist to locate the number of Juanita Guzman y Sandoval in Mexico City. The receptionist asked if that would be under G or S. "G," Henri answered, "and please announce my call."

At his desk, Middleton was signaled by his receptionist that "the guest in question" was making another international call.

A servant answered the call and the receptionist asked, in a Castilian dialect, if Madame Juanita Guzman y Sandoval was available to receive a call from Henri La Fontaine. When an old lady answered, "Henri?" the receptionist closed the connection so that they could speak privately.

Henri told the old lady that he had called to wish her a happy birthday. She was under the impression, she said, that her birthday was not due for another month or two, around Christmas time. Then, he said, she should regard his call as anticipatory…. he was extending his felicitations in advance. She was not entirely sure which of her many relatives this particular Henri was, but she knew that everyone would be so happy to hear that he was in good health and as well-mannered as always. He asked her how all her loved-ones were, and she replied that she had just seen them at a dinner party. She thanked him for asking about them and said she would convey his regards. Henri told her that it was wonderful to have heard her voice again. "Adios, votre Altesse." He hung up.

"The old bitch is senile… thank God," he mumbled.

He picked up the phone and in a tremulous voice asked the receptionist to connect him to Alonzo Griffin in Buenos Aires and to announce the call. Griffin was a retired engineer who had once worked at *Les Falaises* in Martinique. When he answered and said that of course, he was available to speak to his Lordship, Henri got on the line and told him of a horrible dream he had just had about him and he wanted to be sure - however idiotic it seemed - that he was all right. Naturally, Griffin wanted to know what the dream was, and Henri related a bizarre scenario in which Griffin had avoided being shot by deciding, at the very last minute, not to go to the theater because the letter 'R" was in the title of the play. Griffin gasped, "Dios Mio!" He had recently been invited to attend a production of *The Importance of Being Ernest* and there definitely was an R in that. Two in fact. Now, thanks to Henri's kindness, he would decline the invitation. He thanked Henri for taking the trouble to inform him of this most peculiar and possibly prescient dream. As loving friends, they said goodbye.

During Henri's desperate third call, to a friend in Austria, he inquired about global warming. He said that he had wanted to invest in some sea side property, and he wanted honest information - not the puffery of real estate agents. What was the latest information circulated among the conoscenti about the rise in the Atlantic's water level? He listened patiently to the latest gossip about Norwegian land values and computer hackers. Henri thanked his friend profusely and said he'd see him in a few months.

He spoke in a whining whisper as he asked the operator to connect him to Karl van Doorn of Honolulu. Honolulu was six hours behind. Well, the old man rose at dawn. If he awakened him a little earlier it couldn't be helped. 'Uncle Karl' was actually a relative of Joeren van Doorn of The Hague, an old and trusted family friend. The old man had to be told by the operator several times who it was who was calling him in the 'middle of the night,' but when he determined who his caller was, he enthusiastically agreed to speak to him. Henri talked to him about volcanoes and tsunamis and the wonderful things that a person could find washed up on the beach. After ten minutes of discussing the marvels of flotsam and jetsam, Henri concluded the call.

"That ought to do it," Henri announced, and Martin agreed.

John Middleton spoke to the receptionist and obtained the destination of the four calls La Fontaine had just made. He quickly called Everett Smith. While they spoke, Smith's phone clicked 'call waiting.' "Let me get this, John. I'll get back to you later."

Everett Smith knew what was coming but acted surprised.

Henri prepared his voice to sound completely stressed. "Something terrible has happened. I must talk to you. I...I... I don't know.. I don't know where to begin. I can't talk. I received more photographs of

Lilyanne. And more threats. Will you meet me at that Lieutenant Long's place again."

Everett didn't know what to say. At the sound of "more photographs" his heart had stopped beating. Now he found himself saying, "Yes, I'll leave now."

Henri immediately rubbed hand lotion into his eyes and followed Eric down to the garage.

At the Inn, Henri sat at the same table he and Everett had used the previous week.

Everett Smith entered the bar to see Henri sitting in a booth, holding his hands over his face, and leaning on his elbows. A manila envelope lay on the table.

"What happened?" Everett asked.

Henri looked up and then shoved the manila envelope to the other side of the table as Everett sat down. Everett looked directly at the five photographs and groaned. He read the letter. "Have you complied?"

"I tried to. I didn't get the envelope until yesterday afternoon but then the bank was closed in Vienna. I tried to find out from the bank in the Cayman Islands when they got the six hundred thousand, but they wouldn't tell me anything. And then I went ahead and sent faxes authorizing the transfer to the charity account in the Caymans but this morning, first thing, the hotel manager showed me these faxes that had come in through the night." He produced the faxes.

"So your mother has emptied your account. There is no doubting that she does not want this wedding to take place. I can't say that I blame her. You know and I know that the photographs are phony, but what is a mother to do? Even my own wife refuses to participate in the ceremony."

"I can't believe my mother would do this to me." Henri eyes were puffy and red. There was no doubt that he had been crying for hours. "My God. My God," he moaned. "This was supposed to be the happiest time of my life. I called people… hah… good friends when they need you, but not so good when you need them! I asked for a loan… and I know that they have the money. But the answer was the same. I called Mexico

City... Buenos Aires... Vienna... Honolulu. I am beyond humiliation. My God! My God!"

Everett could barely speak. "We can't let these photographs be seen by anyone. The letter... it was signed by GTC. Is that the person's initials?"

"No, it could be one of dozens of men I went to school with. We would 'hang out' - I guess is the term - at a tavern. We called it a club, but it wasn't a club. GTC stands for Good Time Charlies. It's stupid, I know. My God, what am I to do? Please don't tell Lilyanne about any of this. Please. I don't care what it looks like, I know that she had to have been drugged or hypnotized or something... threatened..." He wiped his eyes and blew his nose.

"Easy, son," said Everett. "We can settle this like men. People like us are always under attack by people who want to get rich quick. Don't worry. We'll pay."

"I want to go ahead with the nuptials. If you don't want a high mass, we can get married at the altar of a small church. I don't want to wait. I can't take much more of this. Do you object to our having a small, intimate wedding at the church?"

"We have a problem. The six hundred I sent came out of a private account. Sending more money, especially a sum like this, will require my wife's signature. There's another deadline, I see. And I don't know that I can pull this off in good time. She's in Cape May. And she's not taking my calls."

Henri had not counted on this development. "I'll do anything you tell me to do, anything that you think would help."

"My broker will sell if she faxes him her authority obtained under a notary's seal. But the deadline is February 5th. Today is the third. I can try to call her again. Sit tight." He got out his cellphone. "I'll try again." Smith's call went to voice-mail. "My car is outside. My man knows the fastest way to get down there. Do you want to go and see what we can accomplish confronting her directly? I'll tell her the money is for a wedding present. What can you think of that costs $750K?"

"Property... land. You can say it's for a parcel of land that we've wanted that adjoins our estate in France. We own the entire valley so no one can dispute it. And it will be Lily's land, too. I am an only child."

They left the Inn without even ordering a drink.

Cecelia Smith was miserable in Cape May. Snow had fallen, and while seeing snow fall on the beach and into the surf had a novel attraction, it was not a sustaining one. She turned away from the window and called the caretaker to bring more wood for the fireplace. She had been uneasy, and staring into the fire helped to bring clarity to her muddled thoughts. "I cannot become a prisoner of my own feelings," she whispered to herself. "I have to look at this monster objectively. Too much is just too coincidental. Somehow, some way, Henri and his miserable mother are connected to this treachery. The pictures, the jewelry, the blackmail demand, the private wedding, the reception being held at some indefinite time in the future... the complete lack of dates.. dates that I could tell my friends about... everything was nebulous except the extortion demand... that had a very definite date!"

Why would Henri want to marry Lilyanne after seeing those photographs? It was beyond comprehension. Why didn't he leave with his mother? "I would have!" she said aloud. Come to think of it, she would have done exactly what Charlotte did. One look at those photographs and she'd be gone. Henri barely knew the girl. He was handsome, titled, intelligent, rich. But, but.. damn it all, *he was serious enough for his mother to check up on her family.* That was important. He was obviously in love enough for that wretched woman to engage private investigators. "I should have been the one to investigate *them.* If only I had followed my instincts about that uneducated woman. Oh, I knew it! I was suspicious of her when we talked at that party in Washington and all she could give by way of her academic background was 'private tutors.' Who knows what kind of friends a young woman picks up when she does not travel in proper academic societies." She picked up the poker and stabbed a log. But what could she do about anything? How could she stop it? The wedding now had the momentum of a runaway train.

She walked to the mail box. There was only one piece of mail in it: an invitation to join a local yoga class. She called the phone number and was told that the bus that routinely passed her property would take her directly to the yoga studio. And if she needed garments and a mat, they had a nice selection for sale there. Why didn't she come for the afternoon class. It's for a younger group of women, business women and such. Or, if you prefer, we have a class for young mothers and also several classes for the elderly. "I'll be there this afternoon," Cecelia said. "I'll come early so that I can properly outfit myself." The bus would come by at 3:15 p.m. She notified her housekeeper that she would be out for the afternoon. She turned her cellphone off and tossed it into a drawer. She bathed and dressed casually. This was a new beginning. She would be the best yoga student Cape May had ever seen. A bus! How long had it been since she had taken a bus? She already felt ten years younger just thinking about the adventure.

Lilyanne Smith wanted to buy her wedding gown and she wanted her mother to be there with her to help her pick it out. She went to the kitchen to ask Sanford if he had heard anything about her mother's return.

"No, not a word," said Sanford, seeing the bewilderment in Lilyanne's eyes. "Call your mother in Cape May and ask her," he suggested.

"What if she's still mad at me? I've left messages on her cellphone, but she hasn't returned my calls and the house's landline phone has been disconnected for the season."

The cook was listening. "Call the caretaker. You can try Mr. Kambouris' private line. I have it here. Maybe your mother put her cellphone in a drawer. You know how she hates talking on a cellphone." She opened her address book and read to Sanford the caretaker's number.

Sanford placed the call. "We can at least find out if she is in residence there." He handed the phone to Lilyanne.

Mr. Kambouris was happy to speak to Lilyanne. He remembered her as a child, he said. She asked, "Is my mother at home there?"

"No," Kambouris said. "I just saw her walking to the bus stop. I wasn't surprised. She's very independent. But it is a pleasure to have her here with us again." Did she want him to give her a message? Lilyanne said that she didn't and was sorry to have disturbed him.

Sanford took the phone. "Listen Doug, give me a call back the moment you see Mrs. Smith. You don't have to tell her I called. Just call me to let me know that she's all right so that we can stop worrying."

Lilyanne continued to cry. "Letty," Sanford directed the cook, "she could use some mothering. Take care of it. I have an important call to make."

Sanford wanted to talk to George Wagner who, at the moment, was trying to mediate a bickering session between the Japanese designer and the general contractor who was making the alterations. He called George's cellphone and his office phone. But his calls went to voice-mail.

At the office, Beryl picked up the phone messages. She noted Sanford's call. She called George. His phone was still shut off. She got into her car and drove to his house.

At 4 p.m. the Smith limo pulled into the driveway of their Cape May home. The weather had turned cold. The forecast was for more snow.

Throughout the hour and a half drive, the two men did not speak. Henri did not know what to say and Everett was too disconsolate after seeing the latest group of five pornographic photographs of his daughter to say a word.

The housekeeper had kept the fire burning brightly in the living room. They went in and were told that Mrs. Smith had gone out without telling anyone where she was headed. She had taken a public bus. "My God," Smith said. "I have no idea what this could mean. A bus?"

They ordered two bourbons and sat in the living room as though they were keeping vigil. At five o'clock the businesses would close and there was no possibility that any transfer of funds could be accomplished that day.

By five o'clock they had finished three bourbons. "Are you hungry?" Henri asked.

"No," Smith said.

"Neither am I. Would another bourbon be in order?"

"Another ten bourbons would be in order," said Everett and told the housekeeper to leave the bottle on the table.

George Wagner called Sanford immediately. "What's up?"

"I don't know what all is going on, but something terrible is happening. There was a meeting between Mr. Smith and his Lordship and Mr. Smith sent six hundred thousand dollars to Europe. And then there was another one of those 'meet me at the Inn' emergencies. Then they just didn't come home. The chauffeur called to say that they went directly to Cape May. Mr. Smith would need to get Madam's signature on any large transfer of money."

"Sanford," George pleaded, "I don't know what you're talking about. And I'm off the case. I have no right to interfere in this."

"Can I engage you?"

"Why would you want to? What's going on?"

"On the night Lily was attacked, she was photographed in obscene poses--"

"What?"

"I don't know what's going on. I can show you. The pictures are fakes... or else she was drugged... I can't tell. I'd send the pictures to you by the computer but I really don't know how to operate the thing. Can you and Beryl come out here and copy these pictures to examine them? There are three, one worse than the next. And there's a blackmail letter and faxes of money transfers. Six hundred thousand dollars. For that kind of money, people will kill. Please, George... for the girl's sake."

"We can come out there and scan the photos. We'll need high resolution scans for forensic purposes. Can you arrange to get us private time in the hothouse?"

"I think the bride and groom are supposed to have lunch here tomorrow. I'll know more when Mr. Smith gets home."

"I'll need a signed contract," George said. "That Countess is a wily creature. We have to do things strictly by the book."

"Yes… yes… I agree. Bring the documents with you and I'll sign them and give you your retainer."

"A dollar, Sanford. I'll need a dollar."

Cecelia Smith, a newly converted health zealot, stopped at a market and entered her home with a shopping bag of cottage cheese, vegetables, pita bread, and butter that required immediate clarification. She went directly to the kitchen's side door and instructed the housekeeper in the art of making ghee. "Steam these veggies," she said. "I'm going to bathe and change my clothes."

"Madam," the housekeeper said, "you might first want to stop in the living room."

"I'm not blind. I saw Mr. Smith's limo outside. I will pretend that I did not see it." She went up the back stairs. Not until they heard the water pipes clang did Everett and Henri know that she had returned home.

The caretaker noted her arrival and called Sanford. "She's here and Smith's here and a young blonde guy is with him."

Sanford thanked him. He knew who was there, but he did not know what it meant.

A half hour later she entered the room wearing a white batiste garment in a style worn in Kerala. "You're both drunk. Leave this house immediately."

"For God's sake, Cecelia! Stop this charade." Everett Smith had evidently chosen the wrong approach, although it was doubtful that any approach would have succeeded.

"You are filling the air with the pheromones of hostility. Now I shall have to air out the room to be rid of the stench of two drunks. More wood must be burned. Think of the carbon footprint. Now… Leave!"

"I'm not goin' anywhere." Smith slurred the words.

"If I must summon the police, I will. I'll count to five and then you had better be gone. *Eka, do, tina, cara, panca.*" Cecelia had learned to count to five (and no higher) in Hindi at the yoga studio.

Henri stood up. "We're doomed, anyway, Ev. You wanna go up to Atlantic City and try to be the guys who broke the bank at Monte Carlo?"

As Everett began to sing in English, "As I walk along the Bois Boolong," Henri simultaneously sang, "*Comme je marche le long du Bois Boolong,*" which struck the two men inordinately funny. Henri then continued in English and they left the house singing, "With an independent air, you can hear the girls declare, he must be a millionaire…"

Cecelia Tarleton Smith sat down and wept uncontrollably.

They did not go north to Atlantic City but instead drove home.

On their way, Henri called Eric and told him to pick him up shortly at Tarleton's gate.

THURSDAY, FEBRUARY 4, 2010

In the morning, Sanford took two manila envelopes from Smith's desk. He opened them and looked at the photographs and the demands for money. His chin quivered and he returned the envelopes to the desk drawer.

Smith had breakfast in his study. As Sanford set the tray down on his desk, Smith asked, "Have you seen my daughter this morning?"

"Yes, sir. She is in the kitchen. Crying."

Smith finished his meal and carried his own tray down to the kitchen.

Lilyanne was sitting on Letty's lap, sobbing in her arms. As Everett entered the room, Lilyanne stopped crying and the cook glared at him. "Why isn't Madam at home," Letty said, "and don't tell me that it is no concern of mine."

Smith passively regarded the cook's question. "She's involved in a dispute with the groom's mother. She has some papers to sign and she refuses to sign them. We'll have to get along without her."

"How can a bride get married without her mother?" Letty demanded to know.

"Letty, she will not talk to me. I cannot convince her of anything. Call her if you feel so powerful that you think you can make a difference."

Letty commanded Sanford. "Hand me your phone and my address book."

She called the housekeeper's private line in Cape May. "Put Madam on the phone!" she ordered, skipping all pleasantries.

Letty's entire demeanor changed when Cecelia answered. "Madam, please don't be angry with me but there is something that I must tell you.

The gossip has already begun. At the market this morning, a newspaper person was trying to discover why a society matron of your station was not attending to her only child's needs at such a crucial time as a wedding. I could see on the faces of those around us that they were shocked to think that you would abandon a girl who left a convent at your request after Everett Junior's death. Then she turned to me and said, 'By the way, what's the skinny on the Everett boy?' That's what she called digging for dirt... 'the skinny.'

"Madam, it isn't only common folk who pry into private lives. The Tarletons are historically important. There are historians now who are looking for something sensational to write about, something that will make a name for themselves. If you are angry with Miss Lilyanne, you have your reasons and they're none of my business. But Madam, historians will say that *it is their business* to discover the reasons and they will lie and exaggerate as suits their appetite for scandal mongering. My heart sank in the market when that writer wanted to dig dirt on that dear boy who deserves to lie in peace. They will gossip with people who were jealous of Everett Junior. They will make up lies and his good name will be smeared forever.

"Madam, don't let evil people sully his name and the name of this good house by doing something so unusual that it begs to be investigated. Please come home. We need you here, now. That's all I have to say. Thank you for listening." She gave Sanford's phone to Everett Smith who was smiling and shaking his head.

He was not surprised to hear his wife ask, "And how do you expect me to get home? I have no car at my disposal."

"Have Kambouris drive you back. I'll make it well worth his while."

At eleven o'clock in the morning, Cecelia Tarleton Smith returned home. She was still wearing one of her new white batiste garments from South India. She was not entirely sure of the reception she would get. If it were true that she was both needed and wanted, the white yoga garments would serve as a "conversation piece" that would initiate a cordial dialogue. If, on the other hand, there was no rapprochement with the principal members of the wedding, she would simply turn around and go back to Cape May and everything would be as it was. She went into the study. "I'm here," she said. "What is it that you want from me? You wouldn't have gone to such trouble for nothing."

"Don't underestimate my love for you. It insults me. Yes, I do need you to sign an order for Jake Kaslan to sell some of our securities." He called Jake Kaslan. The order was faxed immediately.

Cecelia removed it from the machine. She looked at the amount. "Why do you need $750,000.?" she demanded to know.

"It's a wedding present. I wish I could have been more imaginative, but without you the most I could think of was a purchase of some land that adjoins Henri's estate in France. I checked with an old friend of mine at the State Department. It's a legitimate purchase."

Cecelia sneered at him and signed her name. This, clearly, was the only reason she had been asked to come back.. more money for the blackmail. She walked to the door and turned to look at him. "You are a fool," she said. "I'm returning to Cape May now."

Everett returned the fax, called his banker to prepare for the transfer of funds, and telephoned Henri to tell him what had been accomplished.

Henri was neither jubilant nor relieved. Apprehensive, he expressed his fears that the money would not be received in time. "This is all my fault. If I had opened my own bank account as I should have done none of this would have happened. I will repay you as quickly as possible."

Everett said warmly, "Regard it as a wedding present."

Henri tried to laugh. "So, you're giving us a chunk of France, eh? Ah, I don't want to talk about this nightmare anymore. I know that Mrs. Smith is opposed to our wedding... and my mother, too. I don't care. We'll have a small wedding. My bride will wear a white gown. And you, I hope, will give me her hand."

"I will, indeed." Everett was grateful to be reassured that his daughter would be married after all the money the engagement had cost him.

"Thank you, Ev. From the bottom of my heart I thank you." He hesitated, "But there is one more thing..."

Everett held his breath. "What is that?"

"I'm not familiar with procedures here, but don't we need a marriage license of some kind?"

Everett Smith went limp with relief. "Yes, of course. Come here now for lunch. I think that was the plan anyway. Get that license and then come back for something delicious that I'm sure our cook will happily prepare for you. My man will take you two to the county seat. You can get your license there."

They said goodbye. Everett called Sanford, Sanford called George, and Henri called Lilyanne.

Henri arrived at twelve-thirty. Lilyanne was happy to see him and to be going for their marriage license. While Eric sat in the kitchen with the staff, Everett's chauffeur drove them to get their license.

Sanford, anxious to manipulate events so that the hothouse would be available for George and Beryl to scan the photographs, was unusually curt in his directions. He ordered the greenhouse to supply a white orchid centerpiece to be placed as quickly as possible on the table in the enclosed patio - which had no view of the hothouse.

He approached Everett with unusual deference. "Sir, I set the luncheon table for two persons. I didn't think that you intended to be a third person at Miss Lilyanne and his Lordship's lunch today."

Looking up from a newspaper he was reading, Everett replied, "I certainly did not intend to intrude upon them on this happy day, however much I'd like to share it with them. I'll have a sandwich here in my study."

Sanford issued a gentle warning. "Sir, his Lordship is so kind that if he knew you were on the premises he'd insist that you join them, and since Eric is here and can drive you in his Lordship's car, it might be a nice time for you to have lunch at the club and then let the happy couple meet you there for a post prandial liquor."

Everett thought it was an excellent idea. He decided to wear his best casual garments. He showered, dressed, and blow-dried his hair. Admiring himself in the mirror, he decided that he felt better than he had in weeks.

Eric had finished his lunch when Sanford informed him that he was expected at the front of the house since Mr. Smith would be needing him immediately to drive him to his club. "When his Lordship and Miss Lilyanne return with their license and finish their lunch, our driver will take them to the club to meet Mr. Smith for cocktails."

"Certainly," Eric said, rising and slapping a few crumbs off his lap.

With both chauffeurs out of the house, Sanford went into the garage, took the bolt cutter from the tool box and wrapped it in a large towel. He walked through the woods to the end of the path, intending to cut the chain link fence that marked the end of the property. He was not surprised to see that it had already been cut. "Kids!" he said to himself and waved to the pickup parked nearby. He returned to the garage and put the bolt cutter back into the box.

Sanford stopped at the hothouse and directed the new man to pick up large decorative pots he had ordered from a supplier that was thirty miles away. The hothouse man, having been put off schedule by the "emergency" floral arrangement, said that he'd be happy to go, "after lunch." Sanford did not argue. He went outside and called Beryl's cellphone. They would have to wait for at least another hour.

At one o'clock, when Henri and Lilyanne returned with their license, Sanford informed Henri that since his chauffeur had taken Mr. Smith to his club, the Smith's chauffeur would be taking them to join Mr. Smith for cocktails after they had eaten.

At 1:45 p.m., when everyone was safely out of the house, Sanford again called Beryl. "I'm getting the documents now," he said. "I'll meet you in the hothouse." He went to Smith's desk and put the two manila envelopes inside his shirt.

Beryl, dressed as a delivery man, carefully made her way down the narrow path, and in fifteen minutes, she reached the hothouse. As Sanford stood watch near the desk in the anteroom, she plugged in the scanner and laptop and put on latex gloves. She began to scan the photographs at high resolution. She photographed the blackmail letters and faxes with her cellphone camera.

130

As she worked, she glanced around the hothouse. "So this is George's idea of heaven."

"Yes, he enjoyed working here."

"He misses Lilyanne. He bought an orchid that reminds him of her. He keeps it on his kitchen table. "

"The Monja Blanca?"

"Yes! You guessed it. The Monja Blanca." She smiled. "Has anything unusual happened since you talked to George?"

Sanford stood guard in the doorway. "Mrs. Smith has gone back to Cape May and Miss Lilyanne just had lunch with Henri in the enclosed patio. They're meeting Mr. Smith at his club now to celebrate getting their marriage license."

"Has a date been set?" Beryl asked.

"Not that I know of. Her father will be present. That's all I know."

"Did you ever learn how Cecelia found out that George was a P.I.?"

"Only that a man no one had seen before went into the tavern down the road one night and said he was supposed to meet the undercover detective who was working in the Tarleton's greenhouse. He appeared to be drunk and said that he expected to work on a case with him. And from there the news spread until someone told the chambermaid who told Mrs. Smith."

"That is strange… very strange. George had no such appointment. Why would a blackmailer reveal that George was a professional investigator? What about a description of the man?"

"Just that he was slim, in his thirties, and had long stringy blonde hair."

Beryl held up a photo that featured Eric. "Sort of like this guy?" She finished scanning the last image. "I'm done. We'll call you when we've got something." She picked up the equipment and hurried out.

At the club, Everett called his secretary and asked her if she would help his daughter pick out a wedding dress. She agreed to accompany Lilyanne the following morning. "That's set!" Everett declared. "Now you can pick out a bridal bouquet."

When they left the club and returned to Tarleton, Henri asked Everett to help with the orchid selection for the bridal bouquet. Smith, relaxed now and contented with the first meal he could digest in days, watched his daughter and future son-in-law giggle and act like happy children. The money, he decided, was well worth it.

As they entered the hothouse, he said, "I'll review the troops!" Lilyanne squealed happily as Everett, pretending to be a general selecting a man for a special mission, walked up and down the aisles. "Get that flower in line!" he ordered one plant. "Is that what you call a shiny leaf, Sergeant?"

Henri laughed. "You need a saber to threaten them with!"

"Some days," said Everett, "I think I need a flock of goats in here. How long do you think it would take fifty goats to eat all this?"

He selected sprays of a small African orchid from Kenya. Lilyanne and Henri fully approved.

It was not the news that Cecelia Smith wanted to hear when Everett called her that evening. She considered it grotesque that a secretary would assume a mother's rightful place when selecting a wedding gown. "The dress is bound to be vulgar and I'll be stuck with those ugly pictures for the rest of my life," she groused. Alternately, she condemned the wedding and complained that she was not included in the preparations for it.

"You can always come home," Everett suggested.

"I have other things to do here. This wedding is going to be a disaster and the less I have to do with it, the happier I am."

At the office, George and Beryl printed full-sized prints of the photographs and were stunned by the degree of obscenity. "The advantage we have in examining these images," George said, trying to sound objective, "is that we know they are phony. We aren't blinded by emotion. A person who wasn't close to her wouldn't know what to think and *that* doubt would compromise a rational evaluation. Emotions distort everything."

Beryl stared at him. "Listen to yourself, detective. And you are not emotionally involved?" She laughed. "Well, you can study them. I have to clean my apartment and do laundry. I'm sure you can find the evidence of fakery without my help."

The advantage George had assumed that he had, did not materialize. False or true, these were still intimate photographs of a girl for whom he felt an attraction. He studied the eight images but the details quickly blurred. He was exhausted. "I can't look at these any longer," he said, pushing himself away from the desk. "I need sleep and a few stiff drinks."

He called up to Beryl, asking her to come downstairs. She wearily descended the stairs to the office as he announced, "These need to be examined by experts. Where can we put them for safe keeping?"

Beryl looked at him. "They're not plans for a nuclear weapon. Put them in the drawer."

George rejected the suggestion. "We don't know who did this to her. I can't shake off the fear that she's still in danger. And since we have this proof - proof that we can't interpret - someone may want to keep us from figuring it out. There's a lot of money involved in this."

Beryl rolled her eyes heavenward. "I'll take the laptop upstairs with me. You take the photos home with you. They're not likely to kill us both." She hesitated at the foot of the steps that led up to her apartment. "Satisfying curiosity is one thing. But do I have to remind you that technically we are not on a case. All this interest is gratuitous. You're just doing Sanford a favor by looking into the photographs."

"Oh, I forgot to mention, I verbally accepted a retainer from Sanford. We now have a client interested in protecting Lilyanne."

"You forgot? Sanford is so concerned about her that he's willing to pay our fee for God knows how long - just to satisfy *his* curiosity? What the hell is going on with Sanford and you and Lilyanne?"

"Nothing! I said we wouldn't charge him."

"And what about our expenses?"

"I said we'd pay them."

"You are one sick puppy. Then let's hurry up and solve this god forsaken case."

"Look, there are at least four guys who have a part in this. It's bigger than we think."

"George! I've only glanced at the pictures but to me it looks like there are only two men! Have you been taking pain medication? Your judgment is off."

"You're exaggerating," George groused. "Go upstairs and do your chores!" He looked at the men in the pictures. Now that he thought about it, they did have the same physiques. Yes, there could be only two men. But what was the difference? Two or four, they were certainly intimate with the girl… the girl whose eyes were opened but who had to be drugged.

FRIDAY, FEBRUARY 5, 2010

Cecelia Smith could not sleep Thursday night. Finally, she resorted to sleeping pills and awakened at ten thirty Friday morning. She called Tarleton and spoke to the housekeeper who carelessly told her that Mr. Smith and Miss Lilyanne had gone to meet Mr. Smith's secretary to pick out a wedding dress.

Eric was relaxed as he drove to Princeton to mail the last blackmail envelope. He looked forward to relaxing in his home on Cayman Brac and to once again becoming Claus van Aken. When he got to Grand Cayman Island, he'd pick up his mail, buy supplies, and then take his sailboat out of dry dock and sail to Cayman Brac and tie up at his private dock. Or, maybe he'd spend a few weeks with Charlotte on Grand Cayman. Or, while Henri and Martin went boat shopping, he'd bring Charlotte with him to look at that abandoned mining site. The house on it had real potential and there was no view of the sea. Eric had decided that he was tired of looking at water. Ah, he thought, it felt good, indeed, to have to make a choice of pleasures.

For their part, Martin and Henri decided to have a nice quiet dinner together in the suite.

Lilyanne's Irish lace gown had long sleeves and a high collar, with a skirt that flared only slightly; but it was too long and required hemming. She would return for a final fitting on Wednesday the 10th. Everett had wanted her to wear his mother's simple pearl filet that circled her forehead and the pearl earrings that matched it. His secretary suggested that she let her hair cover her ears in a natural look. The veil would be short. She planned to carry a pearl rosary with her white orchid bouquet. She felt beautiful in her gown and prayed that Henri would be proud of her.

Everett's secretary, Miss McManus, told him his daughter was radiantly beautiful in her gown. Tears came to her eyes. Everett thanked her and invited her to the ceremony. He did not, however, know the date. He summoned Sanford to tell him that the next time his Lordship called to speak to Lilyanne, he should first direct the call to him.

When Henri called in the afternoon, Everett spoke to him first. Assuming a buddy-buddy confidential attitude, he said, "Have you any better idea about when the ceremony will take place?"

Henri didn't have any additional information, "I prefer only that it be sooner than later."

Henri and Everett were two men with the same problem: convincing a stubborn woman to return to the project. As they talked, both agreed that it would be best not to send out invitations. Henri summed it up. "No matter what we do we're going to antagonize one or both of them. By the time we have the reception at the Pierre in New York, they may be friends."

"Friends? Here on planet Earth?" They laughed. To Everett, this common problem helped to form a kind of father-son bond. He found himself liking the young man. They had already begun to speak to each other as equals. Ev and Hank. Pals.

Everett thought about the date. "As to giving a 'ball park' date, (a term he had to explain to Henri) - Valentine's Day is coming up. It falls on Sunday, February 14th, so we can forget about that weekend. We could shoot for the following weekend, but that's likely to be taken."

Henri laughed about "shoot for." "Yes," he said, "let's 'aim' for a better day. And weekends are probably already booked at the church." He had an idea. "Since we're keeping it small, with or without the ladies, we can have the ceremony mid-week. We can have it early, right after morning mass. There won't be any competition for the priest's time and I, for one, don't require an organist banging out Lohengrin. Shall we shoot for Wednesday the 17th of February?"

"The 17th of February sounds good to me," said Everett. "A wedding day so close to Valentine's Day. You won't be able to forget your anniversary!" He laughed. "I don't think I have to mark it on my calendar! What good news! Lilyanne will be delighted."

"Wonderful! And as it happens, Eric, my chauffeur, is an extremely talented photographer. I will ask him to take the photographs. I'll try to locate my mother and see if I can't talk her into coming. Since you've been gracious enough to lend me the money for the blackmail, I don't know how she can say no. I'll call Saint Gregory's church to be sure the 17th is available. If so, I'll go by the church and pay the priest in advance for his services and the use of the church.

"I'll call you back when everything is in place. And I also want to call the airlines - how about if we leave for Tobago on the 18th? We can spend our wedding night at a hotel downtown or-" he thought for a moment, "didn't I see an Inn near your country club? The General Beauregard Inn?"

"Yes. Yes," Everett nodded enthusiastically. "That would be perfect."

"I'll take care of all of the reservations and the church. I want to keep busy! I'll also call Tobago. I know the perfect place to take Lil. But first I'd like to say hello to my bride."

"I'll get her for you," Everett said. Since they had not yet put a land-line extension phone in Lilyanne's bedroom, Everett had to go out into the hall to ask Sanford to call her to the phone. Sanford did not tell him that Lilyanne had been standing outside the doorway listening, and then, not a minute before Everett came out to call her, she had an anguished look on her face and signaled Sanford "No!" by putting her index finger to her lips and then wagging her finger sideways, before she ran out of the house.

Sanford, confused by her actions, pretended to have looked unsuccessfully for the girl. Everett told his new friend that the bride-to-be would have to call him later.

SATURDAY, FEBRUARY 6, 2010

Saturday morning Beryl cleaned out her refrigerator which, she observed, had begun to function as some kind of hydroponic station. She dumped zipped bags of slimy green things... parsley, spinach, string beans, and fungi laden cheeses of various sorts, among other former edibles, into a large plastic garbage bag and hauled it to the dumpster behind the building.

She waited as George pulled into the parking lot. He was eager to get started examining the photographs. "I made a list of people who have the equipment and the expertise to expose the 'special effects' in the pictures."

"Then go ahead and call them. This is your case. I'm not doing anything until I finish cleaning my kitchen."

Alone in the office, George began to look up phone numbers. But the pictures in front of him were so graphic that the question of trust became paramount. What if the person he showed the photographs to were to recognize Lily? Or what if the person insisted on keeping the photographs overnight and a clerk copied them? And suppose the person insisted that the pictures were genuine?

Beryl finally came downstairs. "Did you get anyone?" she asked.

"Ah... no. Nobody yet. I'm stymied."

"What's the problem?"

"I don't know if this is such a good idea, showing these pictures to a stranger." George got up and walked back into the little kitchen and splashed cold water on his face. As he dried his face and wiped his eyes, he went to the back door, opened it, and stood outside in the cold. He took several extremely deep breaths and feeling revived, returned to his desk.

Beryl opened her computer. "We don't need a photography expert," she announced, "we need a body expert, somebody who can say, 'In such a position, this muscle should be flexed and it's not.' Just as a photography expert could say, 'Those shadows should be cast at a consistent angle and they are not.' Let's get Sensei down here. Martial artists are familiar with muscles. And you can trust Sensei."

Sensei Percy Wong did not have to be told that the photographs were extremely important to George. He hurried down the street from the little Zen temple to the office.

Sensei put all eight photographs on Beryl's desk. Beryl took notice of Lilyanne's nail polish. "Her nail polish and nail length are identical throughout. And though her hair has been rearranged, it's the same identical length. These photographs were all taken at the same time."

Sensei agreed. "Also, no matter how they've artificially decorated these two guys - stuffed cotton into the blonde guy's cheeks, wigs, tattoos, these are the same two guys throughout."

"There's no doubt in my mind," Beryl said emphatically, "the blonde guy is the chauffeur, Eric."

"I'd say that in these fellatio photos, the man's arm shows flexed muscles. The hand is out of view, but my guess is that he's grasping her hair and holding not only her head in place, but preventing her whole body from collapsing. You need a physical therapy physician - not some personal trainer type, but a real specialist."

"Do you know a good one?" Beryl asked.

"Sure. Should I call him?"

George extended his arm. "Wait. Can you trust this guy?"

Beryl looked meaningfully at Sensei and tried to conceal a smile. "George doesn't want any loose-lipped individuals seeing these pictures."

"Dr. Nichols is discreet," Sensei said, dialing the number. "I've known him for years."

Nichols said that he had office hours until noon, which was minutes away. Sensei stressed the delicacy of the photographs and Nichols, understanding his meaning, told him to have George and Beryl bring the photographs immediately. His staff would be leaving and they could view the photographs in absolute privacy.

Dr. Nichols spread the photographs out on his desk and smiled. "She's unconscious. I'll demonstrate." He went into a back room and came out inflating a balloon. "Look at the girl's hand as she is supposed to be holding his buttock. Are her fingers straight or bent?"

Beryl looked at the photo and began to smile. "Straight."

"Are her fingers pressing in on the flesh or pulling slightly down?"

"Pulling away. You can see his skin sag a little under the weight."

He put some paper towels on the floor. "Can you kneel down on these for me," he asked Beryl.

"All right," he said. "Now press the balloon against my leg."

Beryl curved her fingers and pressed in on the balloon. The indentations in the balloon's skin were obvious.

"In order to grasp," Doctor Nichols said, "you have to flex the fingers and also activate certain muscles in the thumb. In none of these photographs is her thumb flexed. Her hand shows no muscular tension whatsoever. She is not grasping anything. To me it looks as though her fingers are relaxed and have simply been glued to the surface of the man's buttock.

"Furthermore, her body is being supported by clutching her hair. We can't see the grasping hand, but we can see that his biceps, brachioradialis, and carpi are flexed. She's dead weight. Unconscious. You can tell by her eyes, too. When a person looks up, you can see white under the iris. You can't see white when the person is looking down. But in all her shots, no matter where her eyes are directed, you can see white under the iris."

Beryl stood up and took another look at the photos. "In the pictures her eyelids don't move. I saw how red her eyelids were the night these were taken. I think that her eyelids were also glued to stay open," Beryl said.

Doctor Nichols concurred. "That's it. I can give you more, but if you're interested only in showing that the girl is unconscious, you've got enough."

George gathered up the photographs. "What do we owe you, Doc?"

"Nothing," Doctor Nichols replied. "But if you want me to testify or to write out a report about the muscles involved and my scientific reasons for determining that these photographs show faked action, then I'll send you a bill."

Driving back to the office George quietly considered the case. "We have no way of determining where these photos were taken. It could have been on a boat on the Delaware River for all we know."

"I'm glad you're back among the living," Beryl said. "I thought a gypsy gave you one of those love potions."

George was finally grasping the diabolical magnitude of the events of the last few weeks. "Jesus! Think of how all this fits together! One person behind the camera. One person at the opera. And a black guy and a white guy raping an unconscious girl. And the four of them steal her jewels and blackmail her father. This is as vicious a con as I've ever encountered." He continued to think, and then he sighed in complete frustration. "And we have no proof and couldn't use it if we had it - without destroying Lilyanne's life."

SUNDAY, FEBRUARY 7, 2010

After services, sitting at the table in the kitchen at the rear of the office, Beryl and George reviewed the photographs, letters, and faxes with Sensei.

"Where were the letters mailed from?" Sensei asked.

Beryl answered. "Both from Princeton, New Jersey. No return address."

George looked at the photos. "If I had to guess, I'd say that this is a scam that is so polished it has to have been done before."

Sensei nodded. "They used your truck. But how did they get the keys?"

"The night of the engagement party, Eric slept in my room. That's when I first began to feel groggy. He's the one who brought the food from the kitchen. I would have slept through the London Blitz."

Sensei shook his head. "They've got to be the recipients in the Caymans. These people are masters at disguising themselves. They fooled professionals. If they are identified as Christian missionaries in the Caymans what are we supposed to do? Go down and demand that they be arrested? These crooks are too slick. This is a polished operation. And very sophisticated when you consider that to make a copy of George's truck key they'd need anti-theft code-accessing equipment."

"There's another angle we need to look at," Beryl noted. "The venue. They require a specific venue to run this con. What's the one place a lady will wear her jewelry? The opera... and not just any opera... I've gone to see La Boheme and Carmen and the ladies were nicely dressed. But Wagnerian operas get the fox stoles and diamonds especially in the private boxes. When I talked to James Barton the other day, he said that when he talked to Henri during intermission Henri said that he and his mother see Wagner's Ring all over the world. He used a funny alliteration. 'Sidney and Seattle, London and Los Angeles.' Assuming that they're efficient crooks with all the preparation that's needed, they might have hit two cities in the same foray. Let me check the net to see where the Ring was last performed."

Beryl did a quick search of the net and called out, "Bingo! It was given last summer in Seattle!"

"There may be another victim there," George noted. "Check Seattle's society pages."

Sensei smiled. "You'll have to be discreet."

"Wait. Wait. Wait," Beryl said. "What about letting Sanford know? George, you've got a client. This isn't about you and Lily. Let's keep this in perspective. You need to tell him what's going on."

George was reluctant to discuss the case with Sanford. "We've got no real proof. We can say that Charlotte and Henri are a couple of conmen, but we can't show Henri or Charlotte in these pictures. The valet and the chauffeur could have run this con without them. Remember, Sanford rifled his employer's private papers and showed them to someone his wife had fired. He'll lose his job and his reputation because he tried to do the right thing and warn them. And in today's world, the crooks might even wind up suing him and the Smiths."

Sensei sided with Beryl. "I think we should tell him what we're up to and he'll know to say nothing until we're sure one way or the other."

Beryl was searching the internet for all periodicals circulated in the Seattle area. She specifically was interested in those that had a society page.

George, hoping that Sanford could answer the phone in private, called him. Sanford quickly voiced his distress. "I cannot understand what is happening. Miss Lilyanne is locking herself in her room. Mrs. Smith came up for half an hour and returned to Cape May. Mr. Smith is trying to make the best of a bad situation, but he's taking tranquilizers. Only the servants are acting like persons who are preparing for a wedding."

"We think we're onto something," George said, "The money that's been spent is long gone. But what you need to look out for is any new attempts to con money out of Mr. Smith. Stay on top of his activities. These people are slick operators... first class con artists. But we have no hard proof as yet. We're working on it. So say nothing unless the danger is imminent. And Sanford.... Lily could be in danger."

Sanford assured him that he would be vigilant and, if necessary, he would risk being wrong rather than say nothing.

MONDAY, FEBRUARY 8, 2010

Monday morning, the Japanese interior decorator George had hired was ready to begin work. Ordinarily it would have presented an irritating distraction, but now, it enabled him to stay close to the office.

Things were changing fast. George moved into Jack's room of Beryl's apartment.

Beryl believed that she was finally "on to something." She researched the society commentators and columnists of the local periodicals. She expected "news" about the announcement of an engagement but doubted that there would be much about the end of the romance. She found neither.

She got background information on the various columnists so that when she spoke to them she'd be able to speak with a respectful knowledge.

At noon Beryl began to call newspapers in the greater Seattle area, asking to speak to the Society editor. It was not until she spoke to the third editor that she got any information.

"Do you happen to recall," she asked, "late last summer, talk of a local debutante or girl from a wealthy family who was supposed to marry a European nobleman, a blonde aristocratic young man who had a rather imperious mother."

"The Contesse?"

Beryl could hardly breathe hearing the name spoken. "Yes, as a matter of fact. The Contesse de Lisle. I'm supposing that the marriage never took place."

"Yes, I know the story. The bride backed out. It was a sort of 'non-event.'"

"Did you cover the story?" Beryl asked, knowing that there had been no such coverage.

"No, our publisher didn't think there was a point in intruding in what was a private family matter. If she had gone ahead with the wedding we would have given it a lot of space. Or," she added, "if it had been a runaway bride story. But that wasn't it."

"I know you're busy, but can you give me the bride's name?"

"Cioran... Margaret Cioran. It's spelled c-i-o-r-a-n. But they pronounce it sort of like Cheer'n. The family has a big estate just north of here. She dropped out of the social scene after she broke the engagement. Do you have any information about her? As we say, 'Care to share?'"

"I'm a P.I. so I've got client confidentiality issues. But if I get a release I'll give you an exclusive. Is there any way I can contact them?"

"No. None. They do not accept phone calls from anyone except a very few close friends and relatives. You'll probably not get past the front gate." In case Beryl did try, she gave her directions to take from the airport.

Beryl was ecstatic. "I'll be flying out to Seattle as soon as possible. Thanks for the info. I have your number and to whatever extent I can, I will fill you in." She exchanged personal information with the editor and said half-jokingly, "maybe we can "do" lunch."

After making reservations on the Red Eye flight to Seattle that night, she researched the Cioran family. The father, Stephen, was a Romanian-American scientist who made a fortune in electronics. His wife Helena was a well known painter of seascapes and waterfowl. No mention was made of any other family members.

What, she wondered, had happened to poor Margaret.

Charlotte as Beatrix van Aken, a citizen of Suriname, whose sons, Claus and Willem van Aken, were very devout Christians, landed in the Caymans. She supervised moving the Piper into the hangar and took a cab into downtown Georgetown. She casually walked through a crowded public place, entered a restroom, put on a wig, glasses, and inserted denture-caps, changed her blouse and shoes and emerged half an hour later as Harriet Williams without anyone having noticed the change.

She went to the Williams residence, opened the high gates, checked the state of her flower garden as she passed it, and let herself into her kitchen. It always felt good to be home in the Caymans. She turned on the faucets to let the water run clear. It had been in the pipes for weeks.

Mrs. Harriet Williams, wife of Martin Williams, the resident agent and officer of Christian Eleemosynary Actions,(CEA) Ltd. had power of attorney which gave her access to the bank account of the CEA missions. She and Mr. Williams would often host parties at their home for various Caymanian dignitaries and clergymen.

Martin Williams functioned as the group's accountant. He maintained all the records in a bizarre code that only he really understood. The spoils of their various cons were divided into four equal parts. The profit was considerable and everyone was happy with the arrangement. Monies that had been deposited in the CEA account were mostly paid out to a few companies owned by the Van Aken brothers and to the charity's administrators, Harriet and Martin Williams. Their various business interests serviced many African charity outlets. They subcontracted or directly supplied food, clothing, building materials, appliances, religious and educational supplies, medicines, and miscellaneous items, as well as compensation to pastors, kitchen and maintenance workers, and medical caregivers to the African missions, none of which or whom existed.

If it ever happened that an acquaintance recognized one of them on the street, they would explain that they needed the alter egos to avoid all the "free loading" people who wanted to spend time in the Cayman Islands but who did not want to pay for the pleasure. This explanation also served to discourage the acquaintance from supposing that he or she would welcomed at their homes. Otherwise, except when safely alone, they always remained in character.

TUESDAY, FEBRUARY 9, 2010

From her home on Grand Cayman Island, Charlotte, using her disposable cellphone, called Henri at The Declan on his disposable cellphone. "How is everything?" she asked.

"The first two letters were successfully received. Eric took the 3rd envelope yesterday. It should be here within the next couple of days."

"All right. I'll be here. If you need me for anything, just call."

"Don't forget to block in the time I'll need to talk you into coming back for the ceremony on Wednesday, February 17th."

"I'll make sure I'm alone," she said. "But if I can't talk when you call, don't worry, I'll call you back and let you do your pleading."

Henri called Lilyanne several times and each time she gave an excuse for not being able to speak to him. After repeated attempts and a special demand by Everett, she finally answered. "The whole wedding is a lot for a convent girl to digest," she weakly explained.

"Please stay strong, my darling," he said. "I wanted to let you know that I still haven't been able to reach my mother. I will keep trying to contact her. As soon as I succeed, I'll call you. Stay calm, stay true, and remember how much I love you."

Lilyanne was slow to respond. "You sound like you're writing poetry."

"You are my inspiration."

"I'm sure you'll find your mother. I'll say a prayer and ask God to direct you."

"You are my angel. I'll stay here and keep looking... maybe our luck will change and my mother will call."

In the afternoon, as he was being served a late lunch, Henri received a call from his mother on the hotel's land line. Charlotte had decided to go to the beach the next day and didn't want to be disturbed while she spent time alone by the sea. "Did you want to ask me something?" she said.

For the waiter's benefit, he had to speak in character. "But *Mamán*, what mistake did she make! What kind of person would she be if she didn't go to help someone she knew?"

Fearing that someone else might be listening, Charlotte played along. "It isn't as if he were in a lifeboat in the middle of the Atlantic and she were a passing ship, for God's sake. What possible help could that fool need that he would disrupt a performance of *Gotterdammerung*? I tell you she's too young and inexperienced to be your wife. A countess has responsibilities!"

"You are living in the past. Count and countess. What nonsense! Who cares about these obsolete titles? There are new aristocrats in the world… scientists and scholars. Do you think I give a damn about those ridiculous old fossils and their titles? I love the girl. Can't you get that through your head, *Mamán*? I'll take her to Fiji or Bali or some damned place where we can be happy without all this craziness. Being rich and titled is an invitation to jewel thieves and con men. Please don't spoil the day for us. Please. I'm begging you!"

Charlotte quickly capitulated. They had talked long enough to make it appear as though a real attempt at persuasion had been made. "Very well. In case anyone asks, I'll wear my blue wool Ungaro suit and mid-calf coat. I'll see what kind of travel arrangements I can make and I'll let you know."

He thanked his mother profusely and called Everett to tell him that his mother was going to attend the ceremony. "I've told Lilyanne that if this conflict continued, I'd just as soon get married by the first priest we can find. So I'll go ahead and make the arrangements. I delayed until I could talk to my mother. Our future will be so much better with good relationships between us."

Everett couldn't agree more. "I'll call my wife again to tell her that your mother will definitely be there."

"Oh, I forgot. Two things. She said - I wrote it down - she'll wear a blue Ungaro suit and coat. Mrs. Smith might want to know that. And the other thing is that my mother is flying to New York from one of the Caribbean airports. She's staying with friends on their yacht. I'll be going up to New York to meet her at the airport. She'll let me know when she'll be due to arrive. We'll spend the night at the Pierre, and then drive back."

"That is such a relief. Why don't you tell Lily yourself. I know she'll want to hear it from you. And I'll call my wife. What a relief. What a relief!"

Henri spoke to Lilyanne again. "See? A little faith goes a long way," he said. "She finally accepted the fact that you were absolutely innocent. The La Fontaine's are, after all, Defenders of the Faith."

"I'm so happy to hear that she'll be there. Did you make the reservation with the priest?"

"I did, indeed. I was worried that my mother would say she was unable to make it so soon, but she agreed. So we are set to go at 9 a.m. on the 17th."

"And did she approve of the small mid-week church wedding?"

"Frankly, with remembering the night of the opera, I think she was happy to hear me say that there wouldn't be any publicity. Just think... it's a little more than a week from now. I can hardly wait."

"Me, too."

"I hope that now your father can convince your mother to come home."

"This is such good news. I'm sure he'll succeed."

They said goodbye. Henri blew a kiss into the telephone.

Lilyanne then sat at her desk and bowed her head, supporting it with the palms of her hands. In another moment she began to gasp and then, finally, she pressed a pillow against her face and began to weep uncontrollably.

Everett Smith sincerely wanted his wife to return home; but until he learned that Charlotte would be back for the wedding, he had little hope that she would. He had called Cape May every night, but she had refused to answer or to return his call. This time when he called, he left word with the housekeeper that, "the Contesse will be attending the wedding." Cecelia Smith returned the call, launching a polemic about imbeciles who believed in the Divine Right of Kings. She concluded by stating her latest grievance in a dramatically low and sinister voice: the news that his secretary had helped to select the wedding dress "came as a snake bite in an open wound."

When she stopped for air, Everett said, "The Countess will be wearing a blue suit and mid-calf coat by Ungaro. I'm supposed to tell you that. She will be in the photographs… and, of course, if you're not there, I'll be the other parent in the photographs with her." There was a long pause and then he heard his wife say, "I'll think it over and if I decide to return, you'll have to make arrangements to get me. I gave Kambouris a few days off."

Everett knew that Cecelia would never let Charlotte La Fontaine upstage her. Well, he could finally relax. Everything was on track. He could breathe again. Sanford had happily volunteered to drive to Cape May "to fetch" her.

Beryl had not checked any luggage and so was able to rent a car immediately and head north to find the Cioran home.

It was nine o'clock, and the sun was shining in her eyes as she turned east into their driveway. She heard the sound of an oncoming horn and immediately stopped her car. The sedan pulled up along her driver's side so that its rear door window was beside hers. As the other car's window rolled down, she lowered hers; and a man put his head in the opening and said gruffly, "What is it you want here?"

Beryl tried to remain pleasant. "I'm so sorry. The sun was in my eyes and I was unfamiliar with the driveway. I just flew in from Philadelphia to see Miss Margaret Cioran. My name is Beryl Tilson. I'm a private investigator."

"What or whom are you investigating?"

"A couple of aristocratic conmen… a countess and her son… dangerous people." She waited for a response. None came quickly.

Finally, in a voice that sounded strangely distant, the man said, "Drive up to the house."

Beryl drove forward. The sedan turned around and followed her.

She got out of her car and watched as the other car parked beside hers. The man in the back seat opened his door and asked her to get in.

Beryl was cautious. "I'm not entirely comfortable discussing this with you. The victim I wanted to speak to was Miss Margaret Cioran."

"I'm her father."

"Nevertheless, I would like to speak to her. If you want to be present and she has no objection, that would be fine. But the questions I have can be answered only by her, however much anyone else may have been conned by these people."

"You tell me what evidence you have that the people you're referring to are confidence men, and I'll decide whether or not to allow you into my home."

Beryl thought for a moment. "You're not making this any easier. I have photographs that amount to pornographic photos taken of an innocent young woman in Pennsylvania. She's been drugged unconscious, but using instant glue and such they've manipulated her body to make it appear that she's complicit in the activity."

He took a deep breath and held it. "Show me the photos."

"Beryl opened her brief case and removed eight photographs. "Has anything like this ever happened to your daughter?"

Cioran saw the top photo of the eight she extended to him and his hands began to tremble. Perhaps to steady himself, he held the letter-sized photographs in his left hand, fanning them as though they were playing cards. One after the other, he inserted his right hand behind the top photo and bent it forward to reveal fully the one beneath. When he had seen them all he asked, "Who was the man she was engaged to?"

Beryl took Charlotte's calling card and reached across the man to push it into his free right hand. "The son of this woman."

Cioran reacted by staring at his hand as if it had been struck by a mamba and the serpent's neurotoxin had already paralyzed his chest. He made retching noises and his abdomen began to contract repeatedly. He gagged. Knowing what was coming next, Beryl opened the car door and jumped out. Projectile vomit gushed past her. His entire breakfast lay in a line that connected him to her car's rear tire. His face lay upon the seat on which she had been sitting; and he began to mumble an apology. She got a tissue from her purse and handed it to him. He wiped his mouth as his driver came around the back of the car to see if he could help.

Cioran pushed himself into an upright position. He said to his driver, "Help me out." He put the card in his handkerchief pocket and slipped the photographs inside his suit jacket, securing them by pressing his arm against his chest.

It took a moment for Cioran to steady himself on his feet. "Come into the house," he said to Beryl as his driver took his left arm to support him as they walked.

Helena Cioran came rushing towards her husband. "What happened?" she shouted. "Are you all right?"

With a nod, Cioran dismissed the driver and sat down. "I'm fine. Call Margaret. Tell her to come down here immediately."

"Why do you want to see her?" his wife asked.

In a booming voice, he commanded, *"Call Margaret! Now!"*

His wife immediately scampered up the stairs. He turned to Beryl, "Please sit down and forgive me. I've entirely forgotten your name."

"Tilson, Beryl Tilson of Wagner and Tilson, Private Investigators." She handed him a business card.

"My daughter is still in love with that man. In her mind, I deliberately insulted the Contesse by insisting that Henri was the man in the pornographic photos."

"Good grief! That she believed it shows how clever they are."

Helena and Margaret Cioran entered the living room. Margaret moved mechanically and said nothing. Helena tried to sound pleasant. "What's this all about?"

Stephen Cioran gestured to his wife that she sit down and not intrude. "I'll try to explain this rationally," he said to Beryl. "First came the Opera. Henri, Margaret, my wife and I, Charlotte and a member of the British Consulate were supposed to see the entire Ring of the

Nibelung. We saw Das Reingold on a Monday night. We met again to see Die Valkyrie on Tuesday night, but the countess was ill and couldn't attend. We had dinner and then went to the theater. At intermission Margaret felt light headed and Henri took her outside for fresh air.

"Intermission was just about over and the ushers were starting to close the doors. Henri said that while they were in front of the theater a car pulled up and someone Margaret knew beckoned her and she told Henri she'd only be a minute and he should return to the box. He waited on the sidewalk, but then, incredibly, she drove off. He asked several of the attendants to help him look around corners and such for her... but they couldn't find her. He came back to our box and he told us that Margaret had gone off somewhere. He was frantic. She never did come back to the theater." Cioran held a handkerchief to his mouth and retched a few times.

"Let me try to finish this for you," Beryl offered. "Margaret was out most of the night. She doesn't have any recollection of anything. As it happens, she was probably loaded with GHB or Ketamine.. or chloral hydrate. Maybe they also used old fashioned ether, too. So hours later she showed up, dropped off on some corner or outside the estate. She looked and felt as though she had been hit by a truck. Everyone was relieved, but the countess was so indignant that Margaret had showed such bad taste in driving off with a boyfriend, that she had second thoughts about the wedding. Henri convinced her to stay. Oh... was Margaret wearing expensive jewelry?"

"Yes. A necklace, bracelet and earrings," said Helena.

"Probably the biggest stones were switched with good quality fakes."

"Oh, my God! I never looked," Helena said with horror that indicated she had neglected to inspect the jewelry. "With so much going on," she whimpered.

"Are they back in the safe deposit box?" Stephen asked.

"Yes," said Helena. "This shows the measure of our isolation. We haven't needed any jewelry since early last fall... or summer."

Stephen turned to Beryl. "Go on with your recitation of my family's nightmare."

"Well, I would guess that the love birds proceeded with their wedding plans whether Charlotte liked it or not. Just as she was reconciled to the idea, an envelope came… probably to Henri. It contained pornographic photographs of Margaret and her alleged boyfriend and possibly a big African guy. The person who mailed them could have been acting as an anonymous mediator - the other party being an old enemy - probably a religious type - who intended to distribute the photographs to society editors, relatives, and an assortment of people to teach you righteous hypocrites a lesson."

Stephen Cioran put his hands over his face. "He was supposed to be a businessman my grandfather blamed for a crime that he, himself, committed. He hated phony aristocrats, too, and intended to make Henri pay for the sins of my grandfather."

Beryl continued. "But the anonymous mediator - who was supposed to be Henri's good friend, or yours, talked him out of it. Unfortunately the holder of the photographs felt that people of your ilk would not learn a lesson unless you paid… and so you paid.. a million… two million."

"Try three million. $500,000. for each photo and there were six."

Helena looked ill. She asked Beryl, "Have you seen the photos?"

"No, but I bet they were of Margaret in incredibly obscene positions."

Stephen Cioran was still holding the photographs against his chest. He got up unsteadily and crossed the room to give them to his wife who immediately shared them with her daughter.

The two women kept repeating, "It can't be. It can't be."

Margaret looked bewildered. She spoke slowly. "Henri loves me. What does this have to do with him? These are the same men who were in my photographs."

Beryl felt sorry for the girl. "He loves money… and God knows what else, but not you. Think about it. Have you heard from him since?"

Margaret was still confused. "No, but that's my father's fault."

Cioran grunted. "He produced a letter that was supposedly written by me to Charlotte. In it I accused Henri of being the white man in the photos. But go on with the story. "

Margaret carried the photographs to Beryl. "Who is the girl in the photographs?"

"She is the daughter of a rich old society family just outside Philadelphia. She met Henri at the Art Museum. He was instantly in love with her. As the countess says, "She was the first thing he thought about when he awoke in the morning and she was the last thing he thought of when he went to sleep at night--"

"Yes... we know... and he didn't have two consecutive thoughts but that one was about her." Helena slumped back in her chair. "My God in Heaven. How could this have happened?"

"Helena," said Cioran, "get the envelope of photos from the safe. Get them now."

Helena Cioran got up and quietly left the room. Everyone sat silently, listening to her manipulate a combination lock, click open a safe door, and quietly return to the living room with a manila envelope. She gave it to Beryl.

The photographs, except for the face of the girl, were nearly duplicates of the ones that were taken of Lilyanne. Beryl returned them to the envelope. "Is there any chance you'd let me have these to show to her family. They're still being duped," she said. "The wedding is supposed to occur next week. Without the proof of these photos, Charlotte will simply say that your accusations are lies concocted by your family because Margaret was rejected."

Cioran hesitated. "Before we let you have them, or copies of them, I'd like to check your credentials. You understand..."

Beryl took out her license and handed it to him and waited calmly while he called his head of security and asked for an immediate verification.

"Please go on with the story," Helena asked.

"Probably there was no way to determine exactly when the photographs were taken... I mean no *definite* way. They probably messed up her hair and makeup. So the idea that they were taken on the night of the opera could have been disputed. When the countess saw the photographs, she left immediately for Europe or the Caribbean. I can't tell you how Henri finally makes his exit, because he's still seeing the girl in the photos.

Margaret groaned. "I thought he loved me. I thought my father destroyed our relationship."

Beryl grinned at Cioran. "How did you manage to do that?"

He hesitated and then cleared his throat. "In the letter I supposedly sent I said that Henri was a pervert who raped my daughter. Henri showed Margaret the letter. She said he cried like a baby and begged her not to turn against me, her good but mistaken father. But his mother was implacable." He laughed bitterly.

"Was this letter typed?" Beryl asked.

"No. I write in a kind of block printing. It's a style many engineers use. I saw a photocopy of the letter. It was exactly like my writing. I couldn't tell it was a fake. I only knew that I didn't write it."

"How did they get a specimen of your handwriting to copy?"

"I've thought about this and the only thing I can figure is that Margaret kept my cards and notes in a shoe-box kind of case. She told him I sent her all these cute messages in my letters to her when she was a girl at summer camp and for her birthday. He wanted to see them. So she brought out the box."

"And no doubt he took one of the letters."

"Or else he used his cellphone camera and photographed them. He asked Margaret to get him some iced tea with lemon… and she left the room."

Helena sighed. "He said he'd call her again, but he never did. Margaret blamed her father."

Beryl spoke directly to Margaret. "Henri and his mother are con men. Their chauffeur and valet are actually their confederates. This is their M.O. - their method of operating. You will be able to recognize it: they come to town and attend a function that attracts the rich - maybe a horse show or a museum exhibit - maybe they have researched their mark and know exactly where to direct their efforts. Where did you meet him?"

"At a yachting competition," Helena said, nodding. "The countess knew all about sailing. She was with some people from Australia. Nice people."

"Well, yachting is a rich man's sport. The consular official and the Australian were undoubtedly legitimate. These crooks need a way to quell any doubt you might have." She paused, giving them a chance to process the unpleasant news that they had been swindled. "Henri finds his mark. A girl who is not presently attached to a man and who, therefore, is vulnerable. Lonely. In my client's case, the countess hired my partner and me to investigate her family to make sure they were legitimate. Her parents have a famous orchid collection and my partner happens to raise orchids as a hobby."

"I get it," said Helena. "That she would be investigating *them* makes her look legitimate."

"Exactly. Somebody lets the cat out of the bag - that their wealth and social position are being verified, and that information reassures the mark. And who can blame the girl for falling in love with him. I've seen him. He's handsome. Henri wines and dines the girl but he has some excuse for not wanting to publicize their liaison."

Margaret interrupted her, "He said his grandfather was determined to force him to marry some European noblewoman that he personally could not tolerate." She bit her lip. "I can't believe this."

Beryl continued. "They make plans to marry. And then there is some kind of grand social function… a cotillion, a consulate party, an opera. He wants her to be magnificently attired because he wants to show her off and naturally she wears all the jewelry possible. You know the rest. Two of them abduct her and then comes the photography and the blackmail demand. The money goes to the Cayman Islands or another country that has accommodating banking laws, as a donation to a religious organization. And if the countess is checked out, she is legitimate. And her son, too.

"My client's daughter doesn't know about the photographs taken of her. She knows only of the jewelry theft. She bought her bridal gown."

Stephen's cellphone rang. He answered it and was obviously listening to a physical description of Beryl Tilson which he verified to his caller. He listened a minute longer and then satisfied, he said, "Good," and disconnected the call. "You can take the photos," he said to Beryl. "I've had them copied. But fair's fair. May we keep the ones you brought? You have my word I will not copy them or record them in any way. I have much to atone for and they will help me."

"Could you blacken out Margaret's face?" Helena asked.

"No!" Margaret was adamant. "I saw *her* face. She'll know I saw her face. I don't want her to think I'm better than she is... that I should be discreetly hidden while she's out there all alone."

Stephen Cioran asked, "Since all our cards are on the table, I'm wondering who is your client?"

"Ai yai yai," said Beryl. "This is not exactly professional of me, but as you've said, your cards are on the table. My partner worked undercover in their greenhouse and when his cover was blown, he was sacked. And then the extortion letters came and the major domo of their house contacted us. He was alarmed by what he saw."

Cioran was incredulous. "Their butler could afford to engage private detectives?"

"My partner George is sort of infatuated with the girl. For God's sake, do not repeat that! He'd kill me if he knew I thought - much less *said* that! When their butler came to him with his concerns, George accepted a retainer of a dollar. No expenses to be charged. Everybody in the household disliked the countess and adored the girl, who is, frankly, adorable. Their butler got the photos and I sneaked onto the estate with a scanner."

"When are you going back to Pennsylvania?" Margaret asked.

"On the next available flight."

Margaret pleaded. "I want to go with you. I want to talk to her myself. I've been hidden away in this house, ashamed to show my face in public. Sometimes I imagined that Henri would come and throw pebbles at my bedroom window - he did that once - and I wanted to be here to hear them. I was such a fool. Victim isn't the right word. I was stupid.

That poor girl bought a wedding gown! I'll bet she just adores him. I need to help her."

Helena spoke softly to her daughter. "You're taking a variety of medications and your doctor is seriously concerned that you've become too dependent on anti-depressives. You just can't walk away from your therapy. You've lost weight. And it will take months before your beautiful face returns. Let Miss Tilson have the photos to show the girl or her parents. You can speak to her on the phone, if you want."

"And if you went there now, suppose you ran into Henri?" Cioran asked. "You're not prepared for a scene like that."

Margaret nodded her head. "All right. At least I now have a reason to get my strength back and put this nightmare behind me. Please tell 'my sister in heartache' that I'm here and that when she's ready to talk, to please call me."

"I'll tell her that she's got a friend in you." Beryl got out her cellphone. "Time for me to make my reservation home. But first, give me your private cell number and I'll see if we can't get you gals communicating. It will do you both a lot of good." She started to call the airline.

Stephen Cioran roused himself from the combined misery and relief he felt. "No! Please allow me." He took out his cellphone and proceeded to order first class accommodations for her trip across country.

"One more thing," Beryl said, handing Cioran a paper on which she had written her contact's name and phone number. "When you're ready to make a public appearance, you can call this gal... without her I'd never have been able to locate you. The press isn't always fair, but I think she'll do right by you. Tell her I recommended her for the scoop on your return to society."

Beryl left the household feeling that she had had the first completely satisfying day since starting the case.

Shortly after takeoff, she finally received George's call back. She gave him a brief review of the day's events. "I'll give you details when I get home tonight. I think you should privately contact Sanford and bring him up to speed on these developments. Let him decide what to do about his employer."

George had his own news. "This morning Sanford called to tell me that the date of the wedding was Wednesday, February 17th."

"I guess Lilyanne is ecstatic."

"Funny thing," George said, "Sanford thought she'd be 'over the moon' about knowing where and when and who was going to be present for the ceremony. But she wasn't, he said. She stared into space and looked very sad and then closed her eyes and thanked him for telling her. He says that she's been acting weird lately."

"It's been a nerve wracking month for her. Maybe she's just exhausted. Just the same, you need to let Sanford know about the Cioran case. Henri may not be finished milking the Smiths."

It was close to eleven o'clock when Beryl opened her apartment door. She looked in Jack's room and saw George holding a blanket as he slept. She quietly closed the door.

Beryl sat on her bed, pulled off her shoes and pantyhose, and stood up one last time to let her travel clothes drop to the floor. She got under her down quilt and took one deep breath. Then, as she slowly exhaled, she passed into what she would later call "a coma."

WEDNESDAY, FEBRUARY 10, 2010

Beryl and George decided to shower, dress, and eat breakfast before they talked about anything that had to do with the case. They sat in the kitchen behind the office and had a late breakfast of tea and pastries.

"What did Sanford say when you told him?" Beryl asked.

"I didn't reach him. I can't call the house. His line went to voicemail. I just told him to call me. When we finish here we can see if any messages came in." George was in a defeated mood.

"No matter what interests or excites me in any way, " he said, "sooner or later I give it the kiss of death. If I had any idea that renovating my house would turn out to be such a pain in the ass, I'd have sold the place or burned it down." He was having arguments with his decorator. He couldn't convince the man that his bad leg prevented him from living in the bottom third of the room. "He wants me to sleep on the floor, eat on the floor, watch Tv on the floor. On straw mats, yet. But I have to climb steps to get up into my bathtub. The guy is driving me nuts."

"I dealt with the other partner," Beryl said, "the one who was a native San Franciscan. I guess you got the partner who was fresh out of Kyoto."

"Yeah… That's why I need you to come up there and give the guy direction. It's getting so that I don't give a damn about the house. Now there's a landscape architect who wants to talk to me about replacing my chain link fence and other crap. I told him you'd be there today. And before I forget, I kept some modern pieces.. a couple of tables, lamps, and a desk and also some chairs I had before I got married - a Wassily, a Barcelona, and an Eames. The stuff needs new leather, but I thought I'd give them to you. I don't want them. Maybe you could put them in Jack's room."

Beryl thanked him. "I could use some nice constructive work to do. This case is wearing me down. Aside from the wedding, any other news?"

"Ok. The case. Let's listen to the phone messages." Beryl checked her cellphone first. Margaret called from Seattle wanting to make sure Beryl got home safely and also wanted to know if Beryl could give her advice about talking to "the other victim." This message was followed by a breathless line from Lilyanne. "Beryl, I need to talk to you." There were no other messages. Beryl tried to return the call, but Lily's phone was off. Beryl simply said, "Hi, Lil. Talk to you later."

They went into the office. As Beryl made new copies of Lilyanne's photos, Stephen Cioran called to be sure he had the correct address for their office and to let them know that he was sending a check, "just a little something to show my gratitude for the trouble you took in telling us the truth of our situation."

"And now," Beryl said, "since we can't get through to our principals, let's start writing up the case."

George groaned. "No. That's enough for now," he said. "Let's go to my house and see what's going on with the decorator."

They went out the back door and got into his truck.

Everett had taken Lilyanne to the bridal shop to check on the final results of the fitting. They would also be visiting the tailor's shop since Everett had ordered a new grey morning coat and hat and a new suit.

Lilyanne was strangely quiet. She let the salesgirl put the dress on her but she did not primp or pose in front of the large three part mirror. She just stood there without even looking at the back view of the gown. Yet, she looked adorable. He was proud of her. "Can't you smile?" he asked. "Is this what they call 'the bride's jitters'?"

The salesgirl made such a fuss over her, that she finally smiled. "You've done a wonderful job hemming it," she said. "It's just the right length."

Everett Smith beamed. "She's going to be a countess," he said proudly. "My little girl's a big girl now," he said, "a big girl that I'll soon have to call, My Lady."

Sanford and Cecelia began the trip back to Tarleton House. Cecelia was still confused. She had given up trying to make sense from all that was incomprehensible to her. Not a single word was exchanged between them. Sanford played CDs of Mozart concertos and this music was the only sound inside the car.

When Beryl and George arrived at the construction site that was George's house, the decorator was arguing with a contractor about whether a wall was load-bearing or according to the contractor, was merely a partition. George's next door neighbor whose house was built according to the same plans and specs settled the dispute. It was a partition. The contractor was so angry that he had lost so much time "arguing with a fool" that he began to take a sledge hammer to the partition instead of removing the wall board in an orderly way.

For some reason George's injured arm would tremble when he was particularly angry or frustrated. Beryl watched his arm twitch. She saw the expression on his face and the way he was trying to swallow his frothing indignation.

"Let's go home to my place," she said. "I'll make you something good to eat."

While they drove, Beryl again reviewed the Seattle trip. "That poor girl. And her mother put her jewelry away without examining it. In all this time, she's not had a reason to get dressed up and wear jewelry."

George grunted. "And you said they were conned out of three million? Jesus. These people are inhuman. And the girl now has a problem getting off anti-depressives? That's a worse addiction than heroin."

"These people are evil. Pure evil." She sighed. "How are we supposed to handle this? Sanford is our client. Why has he gone silent?"

"We can't let anyone know he's our client. All I'm worried about is how Lilyanne is going to take the news."

"I wonder," Beryl said, "what it is that she wants to discuss with me? I don't like the sound of this at all. Let's get some rest. I'm still jet lagged."

Everett returned with Lilyanne expecting to learn that Henri had called. He was anxious to hear some good news. Maybe both stubborn women had capitulated. Maybe plans for the reception at Tarleton could now begin. But Henri had not called.

He went into his study and called The Declan only to be told by the valet that he had called at an inopportune moment. His lordship was indisposed. Everett could hear Henri shouting in the background, but he could not understand what was being said. "Have him call me as soon as possible," Everett said. Something was clearly wrong.

He sat at his desk and tried to resign himself to catastrophe. The phone rang and he immediately grabbed the receiver. No sooner had he said "Smith here," but that Henri began to groan, "What we feared might happen, has happened. I received another letter. Three more photographs. I don't want to discuss this here. Can you meet me at the Inn?"

"Yes," Everett said. I'll leave immediately."

Henri could barely speak. "I'll bring the letter and photos."

The Inn was crowded with lunch patrons when both men arrived. They would have to wait to be seated.

Henri's eyes, red and swollen, itched unbearably from the lotion. He had used a different brand of lotion and its effect was more than was needed.

"You look like your eyelids were stung by bees," Everett said, trying not to sound too concerned about the young man's obvious distress. "Let's have a drink at the bar until we get seated, and I can see what you've got."

"Things weren't bad enough," Henri said, "but the hotel laundry uses something that my eyes are allergic to. As I wiped my eyes on a hand towel I made it worse. I can't tell you how bad I feel. The envelope came in this afternoon. My man picked up the mail at the desk." He rubbed his eyes with his handkerchief. "I don't even want to think about it." He ordered two whiskeys and put twenty dollars on the bar. He handed the envelope to Everett.

Everett left the photographs inside the envelope. He removed only the letter and read it.

"So," Everett says, "He has hurried his demands probably because he knows that after you're married he'll lose his leverage. He says a 'final 650K.' Notice how he gives us a loose date, until he "takes his flight to Africa.' This man is a criminal of the worst sort."

"Everett… I've gone over this in my mind a thousand times. My school year books are back in Vienna. But even if I saw his picture, I still wouldn't know which friend it was. I'm thirty-one years old. Those GTCs were from when I was still a teenager. He says it's the end. What am I to do?"

"I've never dealt with a blackmailer." Everett made sure no one was looking over his shoulder and looked at the photographs. "My God. These are horrible." He pushed the photographs back into the envelope. "I called my broker and my banker. He replaced the money you sent from your account and he sent them $750K. I'll have to find a way to get my wife to sign an order to sell. We'll get them that 650K and then that will have to be the end of it."

"Sir… I've been thinking. I want two things. Please don't be shocked by what I'm telling you. Please, I'm asking you to see this from my point of view. First, I want to take Lilyanne away to live in the South Pacific, Fiji maybe.. I can get a house there by the beach with lots of flowers. She likes flowers. I'd like to stay there a couple of years at least. When she gets pregnant, I'll bring her back here to have the baby. Other than that, you'll have to come and visit us at least until we're sure there won't be any more letters. The second thing is your assurance that you won't interfere. I have an old acquaintance who was with the French Judicial Police. He's retired now. I did him a few favors once, and he feels indebted to me."

"What will he do?"

"Find out who sent these letters and took these photos and then… you don't need to know what he'll do. I'm telling you because if you hear about some strange Frenchman asking questions… snooping around, talking to friends or business associates, you can think up some excuse, like you've made an investment in a European company that makes a high-security military product. Maybe they want you on the board of directors or something like that."

"I understand. A top-secret security clearance check. I'll get a cover story started as soon as I can." They finished their drink. "Let's go outside. I'm not hungry... unless you are," said Everett.

"No. I haven't eaten since dinner last night but I'm not hungry."

Outside in the daylight, Everett could see even more clearly how swollen Henri's face was and how red his eyes and nose were. He put his hand on the younger man's shoulder. "I'll take care of the blackmail. You take care of the blackmailer." He put the envelope under his arm. "Get some rest. I'll tell Lily we had some "man talk" about honeymoons and Fiji and you'll call her later."

"Everett.... what can I say? You've given me so much.... the most wonderful girl in the world... a future I never thought I'd have. And I will not rest until the scum who did this," he indicated the envelope, "regrets the day he was born. Trust me on this. Meanwhile, I don't know how I can ever thank you."

"You can name your first son after me," said Everett. "And tell your retired police friend to do a thorough job."

Cecelia Smith's cellphone rang as she and Sanford were on the highway back to Tarleton. The husband to whom she was not speaking was calling. She let the call go to voice-mail and then played the message back. "Cecelia... I have negotiated for land near Henri's ancestral home in France. I absolutely need you to meet me at Jake Kaslan's to sign an order for him to sell some of our holdings. I assure you that I will not ask you to sign another order to sell. You have my word. Please try to remember how much I love you and have loved you for many years. Please return this call. It is vital."

She returned the call and, resigned to her own helplessness, agreed to meet him in Jake Kaslan's office. "How much do you want this time?" she asked.

"Six hundred Fifty... thousand. It's a large and beautiful piece of land. It is our wedding present."

Sanford drove her directly to downtown Philadelphia. Stoically, she entered the broker's office and without saying a word to her husband or the broker, signed her name and left. Sanford who had circled the block was surprised to see her standing at the curb so quickly. She asked to be taken to a few couturier houses; but her mind was not in a state that conduced to dress selection. They went home to Tarleton House.

Everett Smith stayed at the broker's office until the funds were transferred to his bank and his banker, who had already prepared the paperwork, sent through the transfer to the CEA. Everett told himself that he was paying a dowry.

Cecelia Smith was coldly determined to learn how much this debacle had cost her. She let herself into Everett's study and went directly to the drawer in which they kept financial records. She did not find what she was looking for and she went to his desk. She took out all three envelopes and emptied the photographs on his desk and began to scream as she looked at the pictures.

Everett Smith could hear her screams as he entered the house. She had locked the study door and Sanford stood helplessly knocking on the door. He had a key, but under the circumstances he thought it best not to use it. Lilyanne and the servants were also in the hall. Smith, determined to enter, unlocked the study door and closed it behind him, but he did not lock it.

"Stop your screaming!" he demanded. "They are fakes. Any fool can see that."

Cecelia screamed, "*What have you done? What have you done?*" It was clear to her at last that they were the victims of a vicious scheme.

"Calm yourself! I did what needed to be done!"

"Needed? You needed to pay those swindlers another million dollars… another two million dollars… plus the jewels they stole. Needed? *You bloody fool! You liar! You lied to me about all this money… a wedding present? This is what you bought your daughter for a wedding present!*" She began to throw everything that was on his desk at him. Calendar. Framed photographs. Pen holder. Pens. Manila envelopes. Fax letters.

Photographs. Glass objects shattered as they hit the wall. "Idiot!" She tore the desk lamp from its socket and threw that at him. "You gullible fool!" She wrenched the Wave radio from its wall socket and hurled it at him. "So enthralled with nobility that you would squander millions for the pleasure of kissing those swindlers' asses!" She opened a drawer and began to throw its contents at him.

Everett Smith advanced towards her and tried to restrain her. She continued to scream hysterically. Tears and mucous ran down her face. "You have made a fool of me... a laughingstock." She pulled another drawer from the desk and threw it at him. "*You have destroyed me! Why don't you take a gun and shoot me... or let me shoot you!*" Frantically, she began to search for Smith's revolver.

Sanford and Lilyanne both entered the study. The remaining servants lined up outside in the hall.

"Here she is!" Cecelia shouted. "Here she is! *The young countess!* You stupid stupid man!"

Lilyanne saw the photographs on the floor. She began to pick them up and stare at them, then she, too, began to scream in horror, "*Why have you kept this from me? Why have you kept this from me?*"

Cecelia answered, shouting, "*Even your wedding has been a disaster! You simpering girl*"

Smith shouted back, "You don't know what you're talking about! You don't know who took those pictures or when they were taken!"

Lilyanne sobbed, "Who took these pictures? Who has seen them?"

Cecelia snarled, "Your Eurotrash swindlers! That's who took them. And your gullible father paid two million dollars for the privilege of having you photographed in these disgusting pictures. Why did you have to leave the opera in the first place? Why did you have to get into a *pickup truck* in front of the opera house?"

Sanford gathered Lilyanne in his arms and tried to pick her up to carry her from the room. Cecelia shouted, "That's right. Get her out of here!"

Smith stood defiantly in front of her. "Get control of yourself! You're acting like a wildwoman... a banshee. Everything is going to be all right.

Henri's a fine young man and he loves our Lily. They will be married and there's nothing you can do about it."

Cecelia Smith was now in a complete rage. "*Are you insane?* Did you really think he was in love with *her?* It was my money he loved! Tarleton money and Tarleton jewels."

Smith again shouted, "Everything will work out! Henri will take Lilyanne to Fiji after the wedding!"

Again, Cecelia began to throw lamps, pictures that hung on the wall, pillows on the couch, figurines.. everything she could pick up as she screamed, '*There will be no wedding. Get this through your stupid head! There will be no wedding! We have been swindled! The jewels were bad enough. But you had to squander two million more on those thieves.*"

Sanford carried Lilyanne out of the house and took her directly to the hothouse. He had not seen that she had put two of the photographs inside her sweater. When she looked at them again in the hothouse and continued to sob uncontrollably, he pulled the photos out of her hands and tore them to pieces. Then she collapsed onto the floor and cried, begging him to leave her alone.

He went out beyond the rhododendron bush and called George. George was, at the moment, trying to mediate another dispute between the Japanese decorator and the general contractor. He left an urgent message. The chambermaid came running towards him. "They want us in the study!" Reluctantly, he left Lily crying among the beautiful orchids.

Smith barked at him. "Put this room back in order! I just called a physician for Mrs. Smith." The housekeeper helped him to take his wife upstairs and try to force tranquilizers down her throat.

Sanford gathered all the blackmail letters and photographs and hid them and then ordered the chambermaid to put the room into some kind of order. He returned to the hothouse to discover that Lily was gone.

The hothouse man said that while the the servants were in the house, the 'butter and egg' man came to make a delivery and he thought he saw Lilyanne get into his truck.

George finally got his message and called. Sanford, frantic and unable to tell the story in a straightforward manner, stammered and repeated himself. George shouted at him, "Take a deep breath and answer my questions."

Sanford gulped. George said, "Are you sure she left the estate?"

"Yes. She's not in her room. She's gone."

George asked. "Do you have the name and number of the 'butter and egg' delivery man?"

"The cook does."

"Then while you stay on the phone with me, go and find the cook and get that number."

Sanford began to walk towards the house when he saw Everett Smith walking briskly towards him. "I've got to go," he said. "I'll call you back."

"Jesus!" George shouted, as he held the dead phone. He turned to Beryl. "Let's go down to Tarleton right now. There's big trouble. Lilyanne found the pictures and ran away."

"Then you leaving to go there is not a good idea."

"Why the hell not?"

"Because you're the one person in this town that she'd run to. Do you want to be on your way there when she is on her way here or to the office?"

He sighed and collapsed against his pickup. "We have to wait for Sanford to call. She wouldn't come here to my house. She'd go to you at the office. And she would call you on your cell."

As they waited, Beryl tried to lighten his mood. "I talked to Alicia Eckersley. Do you remember how she called the Countess a fake? She sensed the evil. And remember... she wondered why the Countess didn't know that Cecelia was a francophile."

"A francophile." He mussed Beryl's hair. She didn't say that... did she?"

"No. I'm showing off."

George waited in agony for an hour before Sanford called back. With Beryl standing over him telling him not to lose his temper and to remain calm and civil, George tried to speak confidently and intelligently. "What is the name and phone number of the delivery man?"

"George, I'm so worried. For a week she's been despondent.... thoroughly depressed. I'm so afraid."

"What are you saying? Do you think she might harm herself?"

"I asked the hothouse man again if he was certain he saw Lilyanne leave with the 'butter and egg' man, and he wasn't sure. So he and I searched the grounds while the cook and the chambermaid searched the house. So I suppose that she really did go with the 'butter and egg' man."

"What is the name and phone number of the 'butter and egg' delivery man?"

"We only know him as Walt."

Beryl stood above George's chair and pointed her finger at him. George asked, "And his phone number?" Beryl put her ear to the phone and wrote down the number.

George checked the time. It was five o'clock. Beryl called Walt and asked him where he had dropped Lilyanne off.

"The train station," he said.

"Did she say where she was going?"

"No, she was crying and I didn't want to pry. There's been a lot going on at Tarleton. I keep my nose clean."

"Which train station did you take her to?"

"Downtown Philadelphia. The Farmer's Market is open at the Reading Terminal so I had to go near there anyway."

"Do you recall the time you dropped her off there?

"It was around 4:15 p.m."

"Thank you, Walt. We appreciate it." She turned to George. "He took her to the train station in downtown Philadelphia. Now, aside from you, and it doesn't look like she's intending to come here, there is West Virginia and the Convent - which I doubt that she would go to under these conditions, or there is Cape May. That is my choice."

"Yes," George agreed. "That's my choice, too. You go and stay at the office and I'll go to Cape May."

Beryl returned to the office and George headed for Cape May, New Jersey, reminding himself constantly not to exceed the speed limit and lose time arguing with a cop.

Beryl had locked the doors to the office and was sitting at her desk when a special delivery truck pulled up to the curb. The envelope was for her. She signed for it and discovered that Stephen Cioran had sent a check for $50,000. In a note he said, "This doesn't cover a fraction of the value of what you did for us. From all of us, Thank you. Steve C. PS Ask the girl's father to give me a call. I'd like to speak to him. I hope it all works out for his daughter. Mine is already starting to mend. Incidentally, they also got a small fortune in diamonds."

Sanford called to tell her that the physician who came to attend Mrs. Smith said that she was verging on a nervous breakdown.

Beryl asked, "Are you sure you don't want us to tell Mr. Smith the truth? The longer you wait, the harder it will be. Where does he think Lilyanne is?"

"She's the least of his worries now. Mrs. Smith is in serious trouble."

"Sanford, can you call George and give him instructions on how to get to the house in Cape May. He's headed there now. I don't even know if he has the house address. He knows to stop into the police department and get directions, but it would be easier if you called him."

As intense as George's trip was, he was still able to speak coherently to Sanford. There was nothing else to do but drive, and so he could converse with him rationally.

Sanford was still undecided about how much of his involvement he should reveal. He knew enough to know that people who have made a mistake look around for someone to blame. "I can't help the girl if I'm no longer working at Tarleton." He decided to act 'under the surface.' "I'll be here if Lily needs me; but I don't want to complicate her life."

George told Sanford in detail all that he knew about Margaret Cioran's experience with Henri La Fontaine. "Look," he said, "you can stay out of this if you really want to. We got that lead about Seattle from James Barton. Beryl followed it up by actually going there and interviewing the victim and her father. Beryl's got the identical set of porno pictures taken with the chauffeur and the valet. So you can be kept out of it. I was on the road to Cape May when you called and gave me the address. So reveal all you want to the Smiths - or reveal none of it. It will work out. We can tell Lilyanne the truth. She's going to be talking to Margaret Cioran. All she needs to know is that you're looking out for her."

Sanford sighed. "She hasn't been happy all week. She's been miserable. She had cried all last night. The chamber maid said her pillow was soaked. She looked terrible and we didn't know why she was so depressed, and seeing those pictures made her so much worse."

"I don't understand why she was so unhappy all week? What could have brought that on?"

The summer house was in the outskirts of Cape May, in an area in which the houses were large and spaced far apart and often had names instead of street numbers. George turned a corner and saw the flashing lights of police cars. He sucked in air in a staccato gasp. He parked. A local police officer turned and looked at him inquisitively.

"I'm George Wagner, a P.I. from Philadelphia. I'm on disability. I was a Lieutenant with the Investigative division with the PPD." As he took his wallet out and showed the officer the identity card, he said, "I'm looking for a young woman, Lilyanne Smith. If this is 2705 Kenwood, this is where she was headed."

"That's the address," the police officer said. "A neighbor saw a flickering light that looked like a flame, so she called to have us check it out. The girl got in, evidently with a key but the electricity was turned off earlier today. She's not home. A neighbor saw her walking towards the beach."

"Which way is the beach?" George asked.

The officer indicated the direction with a turn of his head and a nod. "Three blocks down."

"Is the tide in?"

"Yeah… and it's high."

"Are the blocks long?"

"If you've got leg trouble you'd better drive."

"Nah… I better leave it. I won't be able to drive on the beach. If she comes back, tell her I'm looking for her and I'd appreciate it if she waited for me." He handed the officer his business card.

The beach was empty except for the searchers. George talked to a few of them who said that there were serious rip tides. One said ominously, "If she went into the water and entered one of the currents, she'd never get a chance to change her mind and come back out."

The sea was a vast blackness. The pinpoints of flashlights and their little comet tails of light were all he could see. George asked himself, "If she's not dead where would she go?" The answer came immediately. He walked back to the officers who were still searching the shrubbery on the house property. "Where is the nearest Catholic Church?"

The officer thought a moment. "That would be Saint Andrew's. A mile down, take a left and go another two blocks. You can't miss it."

George got in his truck and followed the directions and parked across the street from the church.

The church door opened noiselessly. He went past the the holy water font and turned into the church. There at the Communion rail was the solitary figure of Lilyanne. George walked to the rail and knelt down beside her.

"What are you doing here?" she asked.

"Looking for a dancing partner."

"Here?"

"Why not? The room's big. The music's usually good."

"You better get me out of here before I start quick-quick-slowing."

"You are in a strangely upbeat mood. I had visions of you trying to swim to Greenland."

He followed her out of the church and guided her to his pickup. "I think you've been in here before," he said, as he opened the door. "You probably don't remember it."

"Are you planning to take any photos?" She got in and buckled her seat belt.

George got behind the wheel and started the engine. "I never take photos." He tapped his forehead. "I keep it all in here. So tell me why you're so calm and rational. I thought you'd be in shock."

"Initially," she explained, "I *was* in shock, days ago. I didn't expect the photos."

"Ok. I'll bite. What shocked you days ago?"

"I heard the date Henri and his mother picked for the wedding. I kept waiting for the big moment, the 'OMG What were we thinking? moment.' But it never came."

"What moment? I don't understand."

"George! Every good Catholic knows that Wednesday, February 17th is Ash Wednesday. And the great Defenders of the Faith certainly ought to be aware of the start of Lent. Nobody is going to be married in a church on Ash Wednesday."

"OMG!" George laughed. "I absolutely never thought of that." He laughed. *"Fer sure!"*

"Then the jewelry. I just had so many doubts about that. At first I thought that maybe this was the reason such a fuss had been made over me and that if he were involved, once he got them, he'd leave. But he didn't. He stayed and gave me that big diamond ring. And I thought it might be possible. Maybe it is for real. And then came the pictures. Have you seen them?"

"Yes. If I talk truthfully to you, will you keep my remarks confidential?" he asked.

"Do you have to ask? Of course, I will."

"Sanford is my client. He was very worried about the pictures. He knew you were drugged. You had to be. But he didn't know who or how or why."

"Sanford saw them and showed you?"

"Eight of them."

"They're horrible."

"You're young."

"They're *not* horrible?"

"It's horrible that you were subjected to such abuse. But if I didn't know it was you, or know that the girl wasn't complicit in the event, that is to say, that the girl in them was unconscious, then they wouldn't be horrible at all. I'm a male person. You're a virginal girl. You don't understand these things."

"Evidently."

"What you don't know is that you've got a sister victim in Seattle who has been suffering since it happened to her last September. Beryl told me that as a secondary wound she - her name is Margaret Cioran - got hooked on anti-depressive medications. Beryl said she was twenty-two and looked like forty-two. Same raunchy photos. Same cast of characters."

"Henri had another victim? Oh, the poor girl! And she's still suffering? She must have really believed in him. I at least had doubts."

"Beryl will fill in the details for you. What's more important is what you'll do now. If you want, I'll drive you right back to Saint Catherine's convent."

"I can't go back there. What if those photographs surfaced? I'd bring disgrace down on the convent. No… I have to get this nightmare behind me and start living a normal social life."

"You know that you can always count on Sanford and me, and your father, too."

"So what is the plan? What am I to say to my mother? She's been like a viper lately. I'm safer in Cape May."

They pulled up to the darkened house. The police car and officer were still there. "I've got our missing resident," George called to the officer. "You can call off the search."

As the officer got on his radio, George escorted Lilyanne into the house that was still lit by a single candle. "Nice place… but a little on the cold side."

"Yes. My mother had the gas and electric turned off."

"And the water."

"I didn't think about that. Well, there goes the bath room and some hot tea."

"You can't stay here. So where do you want me to take you?"

"I was thinking maybe Beryl would let me stay with her for a few days."

"I'm in Jack's room. My house is being renovated. But I can go down to Sensei's place. You remember Sensei."

"Yes," she laughed. "He named me Mizzwong."

"Mizzwong, do you have your cellphone? We have to call Beryl."

Lilyanne Smith sat across the table from George, the light of the single candle cast an angelic glow on her face. George turned away to tell Beryl the news. "Yes," he said finally, "We'll be back at your place in a few hours. Could you clear my stuff out of Jack's room and let Sensei know that I'll be there in his guestroom? You don't have to stay awake and neither does he. I can come in the back way in both places and I promise we'll be quiet... very quiet." He waited another minute and said, "Ciao," and disconnected the call. When he turned back, Lilyanne's face was wet with tears. Her brows were furled and an expression of agony had driven away the angelic sweetness.

George got up and walked to the other side of the table. He knelt on the floor and put his face in Lilyanne's lap. She combed his hair with her fingers. After a few minutes, he reached up and took her hands and kissed them. "My sweet girl," he said. "Do you know that I've never been on a Quest. Never had a single-minded goal. I've got one now. I'm not gonna leave this earth until I get those four devils. I will get each and every one of them. I will be your Champion... your knight without shining armor." He looked up and saw her smiling at him.

"You already are that, Sir Pent. But a knight without shining armor? That doesn't sound appealing."

"All right. For you I will polish my Colt."

"Leave them to heaven, George. I can't bear the thought of you getting harmed trying to avenge me. Who will dance with me then, Sir Pent de Fer de Lance?"

He stood up and pulled her to her feet, and then he put his arms around her and held her tightly. "It's cold in here. At least the pick-up's got a heater."

Sanford called several times before Beryl had any news for him. Finally, at eleven o'clock she was able to tell him that Lilyanne was safe. "George is driving her here now."

"Thank God," Sanford whispered. "By 'here' do you mean the general area or your office?"

"Lilyanne told him that she didn't want to go to Tarleton yet. She wanted to stay with me here. She'll sleep in my son's room. I live above the office, on the second floor. George's house is being renovated, so he's been staying in my son's room. But he'll move his things down the street to the little Zen temple we go to - you remember Sensei, the Buddhist priest - he'll stay with him."

"Then it is time for me to tell the whole story to Mr. Smith. I have to 'face the music' as they say."

"We'll be here. He deserves a complete explanation so you should bring him up here. I can lay everything out for him with those photos of the other victim."

"There is no way to avoid telling him the entire truth. Maybe we can make up a story to tell Mrs. Smith. I've been thinking about that. It's pointless to try to speak to Mrs. Smith now. She's in her own world."

"And also, I think that Mr. Smith ought to speak to Mr. Cioran - the last victim's father. They really both need to talk to each other just as Margaret very much wants to talk to Lilyanne."

"I've been employed by him for many years and I've never deceived him. If he wants to fire me for my part in all this, so be it."

Beryl thought that the office meeting was the wisest course. "The sooner we get this done, the better it will be for Mr. Smith. Bring him up here for coffee tomorrow morning."

"Do you think he'll understand my part in all this?"

Beryl didn't hesitate. "If he's half the man I think he is, he'll be damned grateful to you for caring so much."

THURSDAY, FEBRUARY 11, 2010

Mr. Everett Smith chose to eat his breakfast in his study. Cecelia Smith was in bed, heavily sedated.

Sanford knocked. When he told Sanford to enter, he was not expecting his butler to come in, close the door behind him, and then sit down opposite him on the leather couch.

Sanford spoke with calm assurance. "I have to talk to you about something of importance."

"What is it?"

"Sir, you and I are supposed to have breakfast at the office of Wagner and Tilson."

"The investigators? What are you talking about? I'm having breakfast here."

"We need to talk. Man-to-man. Lily is sleeping now in Beryl Tilson's apartment above their office. George Wagner brought her home last night from Cape May. Miss Tilson went to Seattle to interview Henri LaFontaine's last victim, a girl named Margaret Cioran whose father was conned out of three million dollars by Charlotte LaFontaine and her son, Henri. The chauffeur, Eric, and Henri's valet are the two men who are in the photographs with Lilyanne and were also in practically identical photographs with Margaret Cioran. Miss Tilson has those photographs for you to inspect."

Smith stared at his butler, not knowing the appropriate manner he should take. "I don't believe any of this! I had them checked out by a member of the State Department."

"Since when, Sir, is a member of the State Department automatically immune to deception? These four individuals are confidence men and blackmailers of the worst sort. And now, we have to go to the investigator's office so that you can see for yourself what these criminals do and did."

"You cannot be serious. I'll call Henri right now."

"I just did. He checked out of The Declan early this morning. They're all gone. Steven Cioran would like to speak to you, father-to-father, about your unfortunate daughters. So please satisfy yourself that the birds have flown the coop, so to speak, and let us get on with this tragic episode and bring it to an end."

Defiantly, Everett Smith called The Declan. When he asked for Henri La Fontaine, the desk clerk said, "Henri La Fontaine and his party have checked out of The Declan with no forwarding address. Did you wish to leave a message in the event he calls?"

Smith did not answer. He disconnected the call. "My God," he whined. "Cecelia was right."

Sanford remained calm. "No, Sir. If you will permit an observation, her approval and her disapproval were never accurately based. Madam has regarded herself as the victim and she includes Miss Lilyanne as being among those who have victimized her."

"And what do you have to do with any of this?" Everett Smith was not angry; he was trying to understand.

"I knew that something was wrong. I did not know what it was; but I did know that Mr. Wagner was inordinately fond of Miss Lilyanne and that he would act to protect her. I took certain liberties to give him the information he needed. James Barton supplied the missing piece of the puzzle and Miss Tilson followed up on it and flew to Seattle. I do not regret anything I did and accept full responsibility for my actions. But I think it is time, now, that you and I left. I am needed there because, officially, I am Wagner and Tilson's client."

"You engaged the private investigators to protect my daughter?"

"Yes. I did what I thought best."

Everett Smith stood up. "Then let's go and get to the bottom of this for once and all."

Beryl called George at the temple. "Are you coming down for the Big Reveal?"

"No. I'll pass. I'll go up to the house and check on the progress of the Japanese deconstructionists."

"You don't want to see Lily? I know she wants to see you."

"No. I'm tired and stiff from all that driving last night. And Sensei's guest bed is like one of those Procrustean beds. Besides, I figure I looked as good as I can look when I sat in front of a kindly candle back there in Cape May. I'll have to start taking better care of my face and the rest of me before I make my debut. I'm just not ready to be seen in the glare of morning."

"Don't forget to keep that orchid on your kitchen table out of the cold weather. Bring it back down to Sensei's or put it in the window here."

"Oh, Christ! Something else to worry about. All right. Make my apologies while I go see if it's still alive. People can reach me later."

Lilyanne Smith, sitting up in Jack's bed, and Margaret Cioran had been speaking on the phone for an hour when Smith and Sanford arrived. Beryl knocked on the door. "Your father's downstairs. Is Mr. Cioran available? If so, your dad will probably call him in another half hour."

The girls agreed to talk again after the next segment of "show and tell." Lily went downstairs to find her father staring blankly at the photographs of Margaret Cioran and several "unidentified" men.

"Why are you so calm?" Smith asked his daughter. "These photos are appalling! You were so happy with Henri. To have it end like this? I don't understand!"

"Daddy…. I was prepared. There were too many times that made me doubt everything - but in that strange way that told me he was just too much… too loving… too rehearsed. Sometimes he said things so effusively… as though he were a teen aged boy rather than a man in his thirties. I wasn't experienced with men but I sensed insincerity in him, and I had that nagging, 'Too good to be true' feeling that never left me. So I was prepared.

"And Ohhhh… he was such a Defender of the Faith… such a great religious nobleman. He took his servants to church. *Jeepers Creepers!*

February 17th? *He said that he had made an appointment with the priest to have a church wedding on the morning of Ash Wednesday!*" She began to laugh, not sardonically, but with a genuine amusement. "Daddy… can't you see me kneeling at the altar having the priest lift my veil to put ashes on my forehead? *Really!*"

Smith began to laugh, too. "And me with my formal English morning suit standing in line behind you! And to think I almost ordered a top hat. I would have, too, but they couldn't special order it in time."

"I think Mr. Cioran may have had a similar experience," Beryl said, giving Smith a paper on which she had written Steven Cioran's private phone number. "Why don't you go upstairs and in the privacy of my room - use the land line beside my bed… the phone is right there in front of you when you enter. You can talk to the man without your ear getting hot or the battery running down. He's waiting for your call. The poor man hasn't had a good laugh in more than a year."

Everett Smith walked to the stairway that led up to Beryl's apartment. He stopped for a moment and looked back at Lilyanne. "Now we have to figure out what to tell your mother. Sanford told me that Cioran was swindled out of three million and diamonds. Your mother will feel so snubbed…. those Eurotrash fakers must think the Seattle immigrants are a better class than we are. We were taken for only two million and some emeralds… and your mother's ancestors came over with William Penn!" He laughed all the way up the stairs.

"There's no justice in this world," Beryl said.